The Wayward Apprentice

Jason Vail

The Wayward Apprentice

THE WAYWARD APPRENTICE

Copyright 2010, by Jason Vail

A Hawk Publishing book.

Cover illustration copyright Can Stock Photo Inc./Elena Elisseeva

ISBN: 978-1452876818

Hawk Publishing
Tallahassee, FL 32312

The Wayward Apprentice

ALSO BY JASON VAIL

The Attebrook Family Saga

The Outlaws
The Poisoned Cup

Stephen Attebrook Mysteries

The Wayward Apprentice
Baynard's List
The Dreadful Penance
The Girl in the Ice
Saint Milburgha's Bones
Bad Money
The Bear Wagon
Murder at Broadstowe Manor
The Burned Man
The Corpse at Windsor Bridge
Missing

Lone Star Rising Stories

Lone Star Rising: Voyage of the Wasp
Lone Star Rising: T.S. Wasp and the Heart of Texas

Viking Tales

Snorri's Gold
Saga of the Lost Ship

Martial Arts

Medieval and Renaissance Dagger Combat

September 1262

The Wayward Apprentice

Chapter 1

The messenger of death arrived in the form of a boy dripping wet and covered with mud.

He slipped into the Broken Shield shortly before noon, bringing with him a blast of cold air and rain unwelcome in the warmth and conviviality of the inn. The shock reached all the way to the rear, where Stephen Attebrook contemplated his mutton pie with relish.

Anguish twisted the boy's face almost as much as he twisted his shapeless wool cap. Stephen noted that the inn's proprietress, Edith Wistwode, happened to be near the door, and as it was obvious the boy had not come for the custom and had dirtied her well-swept floor to no profit, she was about to speak sharply, no doubt to send him on his way. But the expression on his face stayed her tongue long enough for him to ask a question.

Edith's response was a solemn glance in Stephen's direction, followed by a finger picking him out of the crowd.

The boy nodded his thanks and made his way around the congestion of tables and benches. Stephen monitored his approach out of the corner of his eye with mounting apprehension. He was comfortable here by the fire with his pie, sheltered from the cold and wet. At times like these, it was almost possible to forget the world's propensity for suffering — or at least to pretend that bad things only happened to other people in faraway places.

The boy, who was in fact sixteen or seventeen and small for that age, reached Stephen's table at last. "Sir," he stammered, "your honor . . . could you please come? He's been found."

Stephen's spoon settled back to the safety of the bowl. It was what he had dreaded. Such a request had only once been put to him, but not on such a dreary, wet morning in the middle of dinner. He wished he could say nothing. But of course that was not possible. He had his duty to do.

Stephen's clerk, Gilbert Wistwode, said not unkindly, "Who's been found, boy?"

"My father," the boy said. He said this flatly, his face rigid. But the slight tremors on his lips told Stephen that he was fighting back tears. Public tears from a man were shameful. One was expected to bear up under adversity, even this.

"And where would we find him?" Gilbert asked.

"South of Ludford on the road to Richards Castle."

"Ah," Gilbert said. "That's too bad."

"Could you come now?" the boy asked plaintively. "I'll show you the way."

"I think we can find the road to Richards Castle without anyone's help," Gilbert said. "You need to get warm and dry, or you'll catch your death." He called one of the inn's girls over and directed her to provide the boy with a towel, a spare shirt and hose, as well as a blanket and a stool to sit before the fire. "Go on, now," he told the boy. "No use going out again in that wet straightaway."

Stephen's reluctance must have showed on his face because Gilbert said drily after the boy had been led away, "He's right, we'll have to go soon so there's hope the finders haven't moved him. Easier to tell what killed him that way. Especially if he was alone."

"Right," Stephen had said, affecting unconcern. Being forced to view a dead man at any time was not something he particularly relished, but even less so right after the day's biggest meal. But duty could not be ignored, and Gilbert made sense. This was only his second corpse, and he had a lot to learn.

As Stephen was about to throw down his napkin and rise, Gilbert grasped his forearm and said, "No need to sacrifice this excellent pie. The fellow will keep long enough for us to finish dinner." Gilbert turned to order mounts saddled for them while they ate so they could be off as soon as they put down their napkins and swilled the dregs of their cider.

Still, the mutton pie didn't taste as good after that.

It had been raining for the last several days and the streets in Ludlow were rivers of mud, churned to a gooey paste by the passage of pedestrians, carts, horses, pigs, cattle, and dogs. These muddy streams were cris-crossed here and there by planks merchants and householders had laid down to avoid having to step in the muck. The hill down Broad Street did not seem so steep in normal times, but in this wet horses' feet often slipped from under them. So Stephen and Gilbert dismounted to avoid the risk of falling and waded down to the town gate.

They walked their mounts across the bridge over the River Teme, up the slope on the opposite bank, and through the little village of Ludford. Although it was the middle of the day, not a soul was about, and the village huddled under the wet like a poor man beneath his cloak.

Despite the fact that the rain had discouraged traffic, the road was little better beyond the village, where it was a sluggish stream with pools in the ruts that reflected a sky so low that Stephen felt he had only to reach up to touch the clouds. Stephen led his Spanish mare onto the verge where the footing was surer on the grass and remounted. The mare pranced, eager for the exercise after having been cooped up in a barn for half a week.

He glanced back at Gilbert, who smiled and waved. He was a short round man with a round face and a short round nose and very little in the way of hair. But he had a quick smile filled with good humor and he didn't seem to care that he was probably one of the worse riders in all of England. He bumped along on his mule, occasionally leaning one way or another as if in danger of falling off, yet he seemed to be enjoying himself. How he could hum a happy little tune on his way to see a dead man in this miserable weather mystified Stephen, whose mood was dark and angry. But it was either this or starve. You had to do what you had to do, as grandfather, who had seen nasty times in his day, had once told him.

They had not gone far when his foot began to itch. It was odd how a foot that wasn't there could itch or feel pain, but it often did. His left foot was missing from the top of the arch forward, yet there were maddening times when the missing parts lanced with pain or itched wildly between ghost toes. He tried imagining that he was scratching the foot. Sometimes that did some good, but not today.

A hundred yards south of Ludford, they came upon three women and a man huddled by the roadside. They were peasants by their dress, thick homespun wool dresses and coats, their reds and blues and greens faded with long wear. One of the women was sitting at the edge of a deep ditch. She looked as though she had been crying. A dead man floated in the ditch beneath her.

"Ah," Gilbert said as they drew up and halted. "We've arrived." He began muttering a prayer in Latin under his breath.

"It seems we have," Stephen said softly. He had seen death before in Spain, mainly in battle. You got used to that kind of death somehow. Dead people became objects, like stones or lengths of timber, and you didn't think about them unless they had been your friends. But he was finding that the solitary useless death that was becoming his unfortunate business left him solemn and sad.

He dismounted, drawing startled glances because he did so to the right rather than the left because of his lost foot.

"No jury yet," Stephen said.

Gilbert slipped his hands into his sleeves. He had forgotten his gloves. "Nobody'll be eager to travel in this wet."

Stephen forgot that he hadn't wanted to come out either. "I don't want to travel in this wet, but that's what we're paid for."

Gilbert smiled. "So we are."

Stephen said to the villagers, "Who found him?"

"Molly here did," the man said. He was short and stocky and smelled like wet manure. He indicated the sitting woman.

9

"He didn't come home last night and she went out to look for him this morning. Found him here."

Stephen knelt by Molly. "Is this true?"

Molly shrugged and nodded.

"I'm sorry," Stephen said.

Molly snorted, as if she didn't care about his condolences.

"What was his name?" Stephen asked.

Molly regarded him a moment with unfriendly eyes. What does she have to be angry at me about? Stephen wondered.

She said, "Patrick."

"God bless his soul, then," Stephen said standing up.

"What he had of one," Molly said. "Can't be sure about that."

"Easy there, now, Molly," one of the women said and patted Molly on the shoulder. "It's over. He's gone to his reward."

"Hope it's to the devil," Molly said. "Hell's where he belongs, the bastard."

"Hush, girl," the woman said. "Don't talk about the dead like that, 'specially not in front of his honor." The woman glanced nervously at Stephen.

"The son-of-a-bitch's good as killed himself — left me and the babes, and his cart's still not paid for!" Molly said with sudden rage. "Left us to starve!"

Stephen understood her anger then. It grew out of fear of the future, of the prospect of poverty and doom. The family's main wage earner was gone and had left debt hanging over them. He wished there was something he could say to her but he couldn't think of anything that would make a difference. Overcome with a sense of his own awkwardness, he brusquely turned to the dead man floating in the ditch.

The body bobbed face down in the muddy water. He wore a tatty brown coat. There was a patch made of green material on one elbow and the fabric on the other was almost worn through. The coat was puffed up in places as if trapping pockets of air. Perhaps that was why he had not sunk out of sight, and in water that muddy it would have been days, maybe even weeks, before he floated to the surface to be found. One hand lay on the far bank as if in a dying effort to reach safety. Even from this distance Stephen could see the nails were dirty and needed cleaning. The man's hair, also brown, floated around his head looking for all the world like a dirty rag in a bucket. A clay tankard bobbed in the water next to the man's head, reminding Stephen absurdly of a fishing float.

A spray of rain suddenly needled his face. He glanced up and down the road, then across the field to Ludford. There was no sign of the jury men. "Wish they'd hurry up," he muttered. "I'd like to get this over with."

Gilbert nodded. "Miserable day for an inquest," he said.

Stephen grinned humorlessly. "Can't write in this wet. Makes the ink run, doesn't it."

Gilbert tapped his temple. "I'll keep it all up here. Don't you worry."

"Every word?"

"Indeed."

"I'll be sure to test you then."

Another spray of rain forced Stephen's decision. He handed his cloak to Gilbert — no sense in getting it soaked — and slipped down the bank. The ditch was not so wide that he couldn't have jumped across it, but since he had lost part of his foot, he didn't trust that he was as nimble as he used to be.

Gilbert gasped in surprise. "Stephen . . . your honor . . . you don't . . . you could wait till the jury get here . . . they could . . ."

"I'm tired of waiting. I want to get this done," Stephen said through gritted teeth, throttling a gasp at the icy water. Water this cold should have brought any drunk rapidly to his senses. But obviously it had done nothing to awaken poor Patrick. To Stephen's relief, the water proved only to be crotch deep at the middle, but that was bad enough. Stephen stayed clear of the body and paused at the opposite bank. Despite the rain overnight, the marks where Patrick had made his descent were still visible as gouges in the wall.

Grasping handfuls of grass, Stephen pulled himself up on the other side. He knelt and scanned the ground as he had often done when tracking Muslim raiders in Spain. Even with the rain, there might still be a sign of his passage. Fortunately, the ground in the field was muddy and a single set of eroded footprints that even a blind man with a cane could have followed zigzagged over the field toward Ludford.

Stephen pointed to the village. "What was he doing over there?"

Molly's mouth turned down in disgust. "He fancied the tavern."

"Johanna's brew house," one of the women offered.

Molly shot the woman a nasty look.

"You live there?" Stephen asked.

"No."

Stephen grew exasperated. Prying information from this woman was like snatching lands from an abbot. "Where do you live?"

"Across the river. Off Frog Lane."

So, outside the Ludlow walls. It was a good place for a poor carter to live. Rents were cheaper than in the town. But if Patrick was heading home from the tavern last night when he fell in the ditch, he was going in the wrong direction, south and west rather than north. Drunkenness, though, might explain why he had lost his way. Stephen had a vision of Patrick stumbling along in the dark, thinking he was heading one way when he actually was going another, toward the ditch, unsuspecting, when abruptly in the dark Patrick put a foot out into space expecting it to meet solid ground . . . and died. Stephen shivered.

Satisfied that there was no sign of anyone at the lip of the ditch who might have helped Patrick take a swim, he eased himself back down the bank. First, he retrieved the floating tankard. He sniffed the contents. There was still ale in the bottom, just enough to keep the tankard upright as it floated but not enough to sink it. He handed the tankard up to Gilbert.

Then Stephen turned his attention to Patrick himself. When he touched the corpse, he found it was as stiff as a plank of wood. Stephen turned Patrick to get a look at him and to move him toward the far bank. Patrick proved to be a big, beefy man, solid and muscular, undoubtedly from lifting barrels and sacks. His brown eyes were open and the lips were parted and slack, which gave him a rather stupid expression. There was no sign of horror or struggle as you might expect from drowning.

Stephen motioned to Gilbert and the peasant man to help him lift the body up to the roadside. Gasping from the effort, Stephen squatted by the dead man, who now lay on his back, one hand projecting in the air to the right, the other reaching above his head.

It was Gilbert who found the wound. The mark was just above the right ear. Patrick's thick hair had concealed it, and ditch water had washed away the blood.

"Foul play?" Gilbert asked professionally.

Stephen looked at the older man sharply. "We'll see."

He slipped back down the bank and crossed the ditch to the spot where Patrick had tumbled in. There was a stone protruding from the side of the bank to the right of where Patrick had fallen. It seemed like an ordinary rock, dark and slick with the rain. Stephen ran his fingers along the stone, which was cold, hard and unforgiving. His fingertips came away tinged with an orangish hue. But this was not the residue of a stone or old paint. Stephen clambered back out of the ditch and showed Gilbert his fingers.

"Hmm," Gilbert grunted. "Amazing there's still any sign of it. Death by misadventure, then?"

"I'd say so, although we'll have to wait until the jury shows up to make a final decision." Stephen turned to the women. "Who's Johanna besides a brew mistress?"

Molly remained sullenly silent. One of the women answered. "Let's just say that Patrick fancied more than her beer."

Stephen and Gilbert exchanged glances as Gilbert helped him into his cloak. It was a story sad in its ordinariness. He could see the outlines of it clearly. Patrick had got drunk, dallied with Johanna, and then set off in the middle of the night for home and lost his way in the dark. They'd know for certain when the jury turned up and filled in the missing details. It was a relief to know that he probably didn't have a homicide on his hands. Just a tragic accident.

From the direction of Ludford, a party of horsemen appeared following a single-horse cart, and across the field a party of men on foot emerged from the trees surrounding the village.

"Ah, at last," murmured Gilbert. "I think our jury has arrived."

"About time," Stephen said, pulling his cloak around him. His stockings and the hem of his shirt were sopping and clammy. He wished he could wring out the stockings, but that would have to wait. He would be glad when he was in dry clothes out of the wet. "I wonder if that's Patrick's cart."

"It would be ironic, wouldn't it — him carted off dead in his own cart?" Gilbert said. "More to the point, I wonder what the value of that rock is. Not enough, surely, to make our trouble worth while."

For a moment, Gilbert's rumination did not make an impression. Then Stephen caught his meaning with a start: the deodand, the fine levied against the instrument of a death. The amount went to the crown, but a small part of it funded the office of the coroner. "It's not worth spit," Stephen said.

"I daresay, probably not even that." Gilbert sighed.

The riders drew up and the cart stopped. The riders dismounted.

"Where's Sir Geoff?" asked one of them, a tall man with reddish hair and beard.

"Sir Geoffrey won't be coming," Stephen said. "I'm his new deputy. You're the jury for this township and parish?"

The tall man spat into a water-filled rut. "Yeah, we are. Wondered when we'd catch sight of you. We heard Old Bucky's gout finally got the better of him."

"He has other business," Stephen said, but the men just laughed.

Gilbert had no need to take down their names, since he knew them all, but he made introductions for Stephen's benefit, adding the names of the last group after they had leaped the ditch with some difficulty to join the meeting.

Stephen motioned to the corpse. "This is Patrick Carter. You may know him. His wife found him drowned in this ditch after apparently drinking last evening at a brew house in Ludford. Have you made inquiry into the facts?"

"We have," the tall red-haired man, whose name was William de Brandone, said formally. Now that the ritual words invoking the coroner's inquest had been spoken, all the men of the jury had grown subdued and respectful.

"Then tell me what you know."

Chapter 2

Stephen spent the morning exercising his three horses and did not return to the Broken Shield until dinner was well underway. The inn's three stories of red-painted timber and whitewashed plaster presented a cheery appearance which stood out in sharp relief from the other houses on Bell Lane. A few tradesmen and apprentices who couldn't get seats inside stood at the counters waiting for their dinners and mugs while others squatted or sat cross-legged against the edges of the street to eat their meals, it being considered bad form to hog a spot at the window.

Gilbert's daughter, Jennie, forced her way through the press at the door, carrying a platter which held half a loaf of bread, a slab of butter, and a steaming bowl of soup, artfully avoiding her younger brother, who slipped by on his way to the yard, only to trip on a customer's outstretch foot and fall. Stephen caught the platter she was carrying, but missed her. She landed with a thump and a curse, followed quickly by a fearful look behind to see if her mother had heard. A pair of apprentices helped her to her feet and dusted her off, eager to have her attention, even if it was only as the result of an accident. No one would call Jennie pretty — she tended to the stout side and had a rather plain face — but she had a lively eye, a winning smile and no shortage of admirers.

"Oh, thanks, sir," she said breathlessly, ignoring the apprentices. "Have you seen Harry?"

"Harry?" Stephen said.

"Yes, it's his dinner you've saved."

"He's by the fence over there," Stephen pointed to a legless man a few feet away by the gate to the inn's yard. Harry had undone himself from his board and was sitting with his leg stumps splayed out, whittling on a small piece of wood. Already its end resembled the figure of a man tugging a noose about his neck. Harry was only a few years older than Stephen, hardly thirty, but with a ratty beard that hung down to his chest, wild hair and crazy blue eyes, he seemed far older.

He had been a free farmer once, but then a cart had rolled over his legs. Gangrene had set in and a barber surgeon amputated both legs above the knee. Most men would have died, but Harry had held on. He was a beggar now.

"I'll take that then." Jennie held her hands out for the platter.

Stephen pulled it out of reach. The puppy-like looks on the faces of the apprentices and their obvious dismay at being ignored amused him, as well as the fact Jennie was determined to keep ignoring them. "I'll give it to him. I can see these gentlemen want a word with you."

"Sir!" Jennie said, startled, because it was so out of the natural order of things for a man like Stephen to serve a beggar.

"Never you mind. Carry on, gentlemen."

The apprentices grinned. One of them took Jennie's arm. She stared at him as if he was a fly who'd landed on her sleeve. Stephen turned toward Harry.

He knelt beside Harry and set down the platter. Harry sniffed at it in a pretty good imitation of Sir Geoff.

"Morning, Harry," Stephen said.

"New job there, governor?" Harry said. "Heard you needed the money."

"I like to keep busy."

"I suppose she'll be wanting coin for that," Harry said.

"You know that's the way Edith works." Edith and Gilbert owned the Broken Shield, or rather Edith did; she had inherited it from her first husband.

"You wouldn't mind making this a donation for me, would you now, Sir Steve? You know, owing to my condition and all."

"I'm broke, Harry. I owe for feed and stabling for my horses, and I haven't a penny."

"Well, you ought to sell one of them," Harry said. "Man like you doesn't need more than one." Then, muttering about the lack of charity in today's world, Harry dug in his belt pouch and came out with a farthing, which he flipped at Stephen.

"You wouldn't be so pinched if you keep going around assessing rocks," Harry said, lifting the platter to his lap and drinking the soup with obvious relish. "The water in that ditch must have been worth something. Why not assess that too, eh?"

"The jury in its wisdom faulted only the rock. I have to make do with what I'm given."

"You know you could always try this line of work." He leaned forward and said in a mock whisper, "Pays pretty well. Just get yourself a cane, show that bad foot 'o yours a little, 'specially on market days when folks come in from the country who don't know you. Like that, see?" He hitched up his stockings, which were only tubes to cover his legs, the feet portion having been cut off, to show his stumps. "People love to see that stuff. And they'll pay for the privilege. Before you know it, you can buy yourself a house, if'n you don't drink up all your wages like I do."

"I think I'll try robbery first."

"Your sort would."

Stephen stood up. "See you, Harry."

"Or you could become one of the sheriff's bailiffs!" Harry shouted at his back. "They're good at robbery and it's legal!"

"Watch yourself crossing the street," Stephen yelled over his shoulder. "You're so short now people can't see you coming."

"Bastard!"

"Bastard yourself," Stephen said softly. Before he'd lost his foot, he'd hardly noticed the Harrys of the world, but now he couldn't pass one by without thinking: that could be me. It was disturbing.

The interior of the inn was long, narrow, and low ceilinged. Stephen, who was a tall leanly muscular man, felt he had to stoop to avoid bumping his head on the cross beams that stood atop a series of supporting pillars that marched toward the great stone fireplace at the rear of the hall. To the left was the bar, a wooden barrier behind which stood kegs of ale and wine. The barrier was there to prevent the customers from serving themselves, as they were known to do in some less high-toned establishments. Here the girls did the tapping and the pouring, and although that commanded an extra charge, nobody minded paying because Edith always chose fine looking girls. The presence of the girls, the fireplace, and the fact of wooden floors rather than bare dirt let you know this was a cut above the ordinary fleabag. And the food wasn't bad either. Ahead and to the right were ranks of trestle tables, all of which Stephen saw were occupied with travelers and a few local men and women who had decided not to eat the main meal of the day at home.

He threaded his way through the tables toward the rear of the hall. He normally ate at a place by the fire, which burned constantly, winter and summer. Today, because it was warm and sunny, all the windows were open to admit the radiant golden light and fresh air.

Gilbert, at a long table between the fire and the stairway, beckoned him over. "Come on, lad," he said as Stephen slid onto the bench beside him. "Join us. We were just talking about you." Gilbert waved a hand to the men opposite him. One was a big handsome man with neatly trimmed brown hair and beard and dark eyes that took Stephen's measure from across the table as if he was weighing a purchase. The man was dressed in a well tailored scarlet coat with a fox fur collar. His strong hands, which grasped a sheet of parchment, were decorated with several expensive looking gold rings. Stephen recognized him as a local merchant but didn't know his name. The man's companion was impressive in his own way with huge shoulders and a thick neck. Gilbert said, "This is Anselin Baynard, master draper. And his bailiff, Clement."

"A pleasure, Master Baynard, Master Clement," Stephen said.

"The pleasure's mine," Baynard said courteously in an accent that Stephen thought hailed from Anglia or Kent, perhaps even London. People had a decidedly odd way of talking in the east. Baynard put down the parchment. Stephen saw it was Gilbert's draft of the report on Patrick the carter's death. Baynard added, "Gilbert was just telling us about your case of yesterday. Sad." He didn't sound sad, though. He sounded as though he was just making polite conversation. "He said you were quite thorough in your inquiries."

"I'm new to the business," Stephen said, "but under Gilbert's guidance I think I'll catch on."

"We hope so," Baynard said. There was a pause and he said, "You were a soldier?"

"I was."

"In France?"

It was an obvious place to go soldiering for an Englishman, because the king fought his wars in France, although there had been problems lately with the Welsh and a simmering dispute between a party of barons and the king that had both sides surreptitiously gathering men. But Stephen said, "No, Spain."

Baynard's eyebrows rose ever so slightly. "So you must have some acquaintance with the Mohammadeans. I would like to hear about them sometime. Master Gilbert tells me you come from a local family . . ."

"My brother holds Hafton manor, which is a day's walk from here, and my cousin is the earl of Shelburgh."

"Ah, one of those Attebrooks. And a younger son, too. A pity to be thrust into the world to make your way without any support." This last was said with some emotion, as if Baynard understood the cold, bitter feeling of being thrown into the world to sink or swim.

Baynard's measuring gaze wandered over Stephen, who grew conscious of the rather threadbare state of his coat and the frayed cuffs and collar of his linen shirt. A casual observer might have taken Baynard for the gentryman and Stephen for the tradesman, instead of the other way around.

Fortunately, Jennie and Paula, another of the serving girls, came over with a tray of sliced mutton covered with rosemary, bread, steamed carrots, and spinach mixed with vinegar, and ale. They put the tray down at the end of the table and lay trenchers and food before the four men. Jennie kissed Gilbert on the top of his bald head. "Don't eat too fast or too much, dad," she said. "You'll get heartburn again."

"Daughters," Gilbert said with fond amusement after she had retreated through the corridor around the end of the fireplace. "They're as bad as wives sometimes. Think they can tell you how to run your life."

Baynard smiled thinly. He began applying butter to his bread, attacking it with such vigor that, while wielding the knife, his left elbow jabbed Clement in the side. "Give me space, man," Baynard snapped and Clement, who did not seem suited for meekness, meekly slid over a half a foot on the bench.

Baynard said to Stephen, "Master Gilbert says you have reservations about the conclusion in this Patrick's death, Master Stephen."

Stephen got his spoon and knife out of his pouch and wiped them off on his stockings before he cut into his mutton, which was so soft it broke apart at a touch. "It seems an accident. But he didn't stay long enough at the brew house to get so drunk that he'd lose his way in the dark like that. That's all."

"But the jury agreed it was an accident."

"They did."

"And you ratified their conclusion."

"Yes."

"The matter should be closed then."

"I suppose it is."

"Ah," Baynard murmured. He tried the mutton. "Excellent, Master Gilbert. So tender, and the spices."

"It's the mint, rosemary and pepper," Gilbert said, his mouth full of mutton as well. "Would you like the salt?" He offered Baynard the salt bowl. Baynard declined but Clement took it and sprinkled some on his butter.

Baynard said, "Sir Stephen, I have a difficulty for which I wondered if I might have your assistance."

"Oh?" Stephen said cautiously.

"I have an apprentice who has run away."

"Peter Bromptone," Clement cut in.

"Yes," Baynard said. "Bromptone. He has three years left on his contract, and I want him back to finish it. Can't tolerate apprentices breaking contracts and running away. It's no way to do business and sets a bad example for the boys who remain if you allow them to pick up and leave whenever they feel like it."

"What's that got to do with me?" Stephen asked.

"I need someone to find him."

"What's wrong with Master Clement here?"

"Oh, I can't spare Clement. Who would manage my affairs? They are quite complicated. No, I thought to hire someone, but there is the problem of trust. You can pay a man to work out of your sight, but you can never be sure he is diligent." Baynard leaned forward and smiled. Despite Baynard's coolness earlier, he now seemed genuinely friendly.

Stephen had a hard time disagreeing with Baynard. He'd had enough experience with men falling asleep when they should have been on guard duty or scouts just riding over a hill and taking a nap instead of trying to find the enemy. He said, "I see. Why not hire one of the sheriff's bailiffs? The Bromptones are a local family. They'll tell the bailiff where he's got to."

"We've a new sheriff now that the king's returned to power, as you know being a king's man yourself, and he's a Bromptone cousin. I can't very well hire one of his bailiffs and expect him to put his best efforts into the search."

Stephen wasn't so sure as Baynard that he was a king's man. He was just trying to do a job. He'd been out of the country when the trouble between King Henry and Simon de Montfort and the barons had blown up. He hadn't been back more than six weeks, and he had yet to take sides in the dispute, although the lines were pretty clearly drawn in this town and countryside. He said cautiously, "And you think I would find him?"

"You come highly recommended."

"How much?" Stephen asked and took another bite of the mutton. It really was delicious.

"I'll pay twelve shillings and expenses."

Stephen nearly spat out his mouth full of mutton. It was a large sum and would tide him over until he got paid proper. Plus expenses, too! He wouldn't have to sell one of his horses. He had three, a Spanish stallion and two mares. They were the only things of value aside from his armor and weapons that he still possessed, and he could not bear the thought of having to sell any of it. People who got that desperate were on the road to beggary, and there was no escape from that. He stirred the sauce on his trencher and tried to appear unconcerned.

"Why are you offering so much?" Stephen asked.

"He owes me money. Three times in debt what I offer you."

"What if I don't find him?" Stephen asked.

Baynard smiled. Stephen had always heard that merchants enjoyed haggling over prices, but Baynard sounded as though making an offer entailed cutting off a finger. "Six shillings if you don't. Six more when I have Bromptone in hand."

"In advance."

Baynard hesitated, then nodded. "Agreed."

"Plus expenses either way."

"Plus expenses either way," Baynard grudged.

"All right, Master Baynard. I'll have to get Sir Geoff's permission to be away. On that condition, I'll undertake your commission." He had almost said, I'm your man, but that would have implied that Baynard was in a superior social position.

"Excellent, Sir Stephen. Excellent." Baynard stood up. Somehow during all the talk, he had cleaned his trencher. "Thanks so much for dinner, Master Gilbert. Your cook is a true artist. Come, Clement, the day is wasting and we have much business."

Clement looked put out, because he still had food on his trencher, but he couldn't very well disobey. He swiped the butt of his bread in the mutton sauce and hurried after Baynard, who was already striding energetically toward the door, calling a greeting here and there to people who knew him.

Gilbert watched both men disappear into the street. He turned back to his trencher and poked the remains of his mutton. "I'll be damned," he said in amazement.

Chapter 3

In that twilight of the mind between sleep and wakefulness, Stephen thought she was there: her scent, like the aroma of a votive candle, filled the air, that combination of lilac and musk which permeated her hair, the signature of her being. The sense of it was so sharp that he came immediately awake, gasping as much with primal desire as grief as piercing as a spear point. His wife, Taresa, wasn't there of course. She had been dead almost six months now, although it seemed like yesterday that he had wrapped her porcelain face in an old linen bed sheet and put her in the hard ground outside Cordoba. Soldiers — indeed most men — had women like they had goblets of wine, and moved on to the next without a second thought or a regret when the first was lost. But Stephen had still not been able to forget her. It made him feel weak and foolish.

He sat up in bed, heart pounding. Naked, he rose from the bed and padded to the table by the window, mindful not to bump his bed against the rafters. The room was on the top floor at the back of the inn, one of the least desirable chambers, and the ceiling slanted so that in parts of it he had to crouch. He couldn't complain, though. In payment of some debt to his cousin, Gilbert and Edith let him have it for nothing.

Dipping his washrag in the bowl on the table, he sponged himself off, head to toe, then washed his hair. He looked forward to the day when he could afford a couple of hours at the bathhouse. Ah, to sit and soak in a hot tub of water, with a cup of wine on the sideboard. The thought made him smile.

When he finished his bath, he eased open the shutters and poured the bath water out the window. It was light enough to see now, and to the right, the stable doors cracked open and Harry emerged, tied to his board. The board was a strange thing. It had little rockers on it rather like those on a rocking chair that allowed him to bend forward so he could more easily reach the ground with his hands. He propelled himself with his fists, which were encased in leather gloves with padding on the knuckles. Harry saw Stephen and waved. "Morning, your honor!" he shouted, not caring if he woke any of the guests, who had not yet begun to show themselves.

"Morning yourself, Harry," Stephen called back.

"I'm off to work! I've still got a crutch you can borrow!"

"Tomorrow. I've got business today."

"It's your loss!"

Harry swung across the yard with surprising swiftness and disappeared from view around the corner of the house. Stephen sat on the window ledge for a moment, savoring the morning. Its chill made his damp skin tingle. Smoke issued from the chimney of the kitchen to the right, but fortunately the breeze carried it away to the east. When he was on campaign, he had always liked the early dawn, when no one stirred yet and everything was quiet, except for the twittering of the birds and the murmuring and muted clatter of the cooks. It was so peaceful, a good moment to gather yourself for the exertions of the day. Then in the yard behind, a woman appeared, headed toward the privy. Stephen ducked quickly back so she couldn't see him and pulled one of the shutters closed.

He got dressed.

Before he went down to breakfast, he paused at the bundle by the door. His lance, a Moorish bow and arrow case, and shield stood there beside it. He bent and untied the bundle. Impulsively, he drew out one of his swords, removed its scabbard and held it loosely, feeling its familiar balance. He turned and executed a few thrusts and figure eight cuts from the wrist. The blade hissed in the air. Then he worked through the guards of the sword as best he could in the constricted space: the ox, the wrath, the plough, the fool, the iron gate, the tail. The sword felt good, like an extension of his arm, as if something that had been missing had been found. He checked the blade and cross for rust at the window, then returned the sword to its scabbard. He had no real use for it now. A cripple like him was not much good at fighting.

He placed the sword back in the bundle, and clumped down the stairway in search of breakfast.

Stephen collected a simple breakfast of cheese and bread from the pantry, which he put in his pack, saddled the older Spanish mare, and headed out Bell Lane to Broad Street. At the city gate down the hill, he saw Harry hard at work, alms bowl on the ground in front of him and hand aloft, beseeching a farmer on his cart who had paused to pay the toll into town. Harry did so well at looking pathetic. Although the sun was hardly a half an hour up, traffic in the street was brisk as people and carts climbed the hill to High Street. There Stephen parted company with most of it, for the corn market, which was just getting underway, lay to the left in the shadow of the castle. Stephen's route took him to the right toward the Galdeford gate, where he passed out of town into the suburb of Galdeford.

Sir Geoff Randall's principal manor lay about eight miles away to the east off the road to Cleobury Mortimer. Stephen considered that it should take about an hour to get there, since the Spanish mare could maintain a trot all day if necessary, and the road had dried and firmed up from the recent rains. Stephen kicked his right foot free from the stirrup and rode without them, as he now was in the habit of doing, since he could not get a grip on the left stirrup with that foot. He lay the ring holding the reins together on the high front pommel of his saddle, let the reins go, and rummaged in the saddlebag for his breakfast, which he ate slowly as he and the horse climbed up the shoulder of the Titterstone Clee hill. There was cart traffic on its way to the market here, too, but the mare easily avoided it without any need for him to direct her, other than an occasional nudge with his leg. She was such a sweet horse and always knew exactly what was wanted.

Presently traffic began to trickle off until Stephen had the road to himself. It was quiet and warm, a glorious sunny morning. Before long the warmth, the sheer pleasantness of the ride, and the feeling that in England he was relatively safe from highway robbers, unlike Spain where danger lurked behind every crag and turn in the road, his mind began to wander.

Then on an abrupt turn on the far side of the Clee he came up unexpectedly on a horse cart headed the other way. Its appearance surprised him and he veered the mare to avoid a collision, for the cart took up the center of the road. It was discourteous to hog the road so, and he almost complained about it. But he saw that one of the drivers was the woman from Ludford, Molly, and the figure beside her he had taken for a man was actually the boy who had brought word of his father's death, handsome enough under a thatch of brown hair. They were hauling wicker baskets full of charcoal.

At the sight of him, Molly spit over the side and reined the cart to a halt.

She looked at Stephen sourly. "Been meaning to come see you," she said. "Got something you should see."

Stephen would rather not have stopped, but it would have been too rude to ignore the woman. He waited patiently while Molly dug behind her into a wool satchel. She retrieved a gray linen shirt, which she held out to him. "Here," she snapped. "Take it."

"What's this about?" Stephen asked, mystified and a little repelled at the shirt, for it had obviously spent some time in muddy water and Molly had not bothered to clean it.

Molly waved the shirt in her hand when Stephen was slow to take it. "You said my Patrick drowned. Well, this gives it the lie."

Curiosity now got the better of his sense of revulsion. Stephen accepted the shirt and spread it out on the horse's withers. "How?" he asked.

"There." Molly pointed to a spot on the front left side.

Stephen smoothed the material. At first, he didn't see what she intended. But then he spotted it: a slit about an inch long surrounded by a crusted patch of brown. The edges of the material had curled back from the slit. Stephen's heart skipped a beat. It was exactly the sort of mark left by the passage of a blade, and the crusted material could only be one thing.

"Was there a wound?" he asked her.

Molly nodded. "Right below the heart. Same size as you see there. We found it when we cleaned him for burial."

"Did anyone else see it?"

"Edgar here did."

The boy nodded his brown head.

"And the parish vicar," Molly added. "Hamo."

"I see," Stephen said heavily.

"You were wrong," Molly spat bitterly. "He wasn't drunk. He didn't fall and drown. He was killed."

"It would seem so." Stephen could hardly contain his dismay. He had thought he had been so thorough and he had missed this. The mistake was inexcusable.

"So what are you going to do about it?"

Stephen felt helpless. "No one saw. The jury made sure of that. Without a witness there's nothing anyone can do."

Molly snorted. "I thought so. You're not interested. You've done your bit and now you're through. The king's justice. Available only to those who can afford it. Paddy may have been Irish, but he had a soul as good as anyone's, better even than most, and he's entitled to justice. Well, you can be damned. I hope you rot in hell — you and my Paddy's murderer!" She snapped the reins and clicked her tongue. The horse started forward, and the cart jolted away.

In deep distress, Stephen watched the cart disappear around a bend. Burning with a sense of failure, he folded the shirt and stuffed it in his saddlebag. Then he turned back to the way toward Sir Geoff's house.

Chapter 4

Stephen had no trouble finding the turn off to Sir Geoffrey's manor. The track was marked at the junction by a large spreading beech tree with a riot of cow parsley around the roots. Stephen remembered it well. He had been here just three weeks ago, when he had come to receive his commission.

He turned the mare up the track, three well worn parallel paths through the forest, two made by the wheels of carts and a center one scuffed out by the horse, and stopped. He swung his left leg over the horse's withers and dropped to the ground. He stretched, surprised at how stiff he was from only an hour's ride. He was getting soft. Town living did that to you.

Leading the horse, he started up the track. The forest pressed in on both sides. He felt as though he was entering a cave. It smelled damp and musty.

Within a few minutes, he emerged into a broad open field. These fields had recently been harvested and a couple of dozen sheep grazed on the stubble. On the other side of the clearing stood the manor, surrounded by an earthen bank and wooden palisade.

Stephen went through the gate. The manor house was big, solid and impressive — three stories tall, made entirely of gray stone and capped by a blue slate roof. Everything seemed neat and tidy, but there was no one about.

He tied his mare to a post at the foot of the stairs and mounted them to the front door, a great arched oaken thing studded with iron nails half the size of his fist. He pounded on the door and after several minutes, one panel cracked open and a white-faced young girl peered out at him.

"Can I help you, sir?" she asked timorously.

"I've come to see Sir Geoffrey," Stephen said.

"Oh. Well, he's gone."

"Where?" Stephen asked. He hoped Sir Geoff was just out on the grounds somewhere and would be back for dinner.

"I'm not sure, really. No one tells me anything. Left day before yesterday."

"What about his wife?" If Stephen couldn't speak to Sir Geoff, his wife would do just as well.

"She's gone too."

That would explain why the place was so quiet. The master and mistress weren't at home and had taken most of the household servants with them leaving only a skeleton staff at the manor.

A thick-jowled man in a new red coat came up behind the girl before Stephen could say anything more. "What's going on, Bess?"

Stephen caught the sharp whiff of wine as the man spoke.

The girl ducked back from the door out of sight. Stephen heard her say, "He's asking after the master, sir."

"All right," the man said, "let me handle him." He turned briskly to Stephen and said, "My lord has gone to Hereford for the sheriff's court and accounting. Don't expect to see him for another week, if we're lucky. I'm Simon, the bailiff here. Any business of Sir Geoffrey's you can transact with me in his absence."

Now that Simon was closer, the whiff of wine had become a veritable cloud, and Stephen could see his eyes were bloodshot and he swayed a bit, despite the fact he had the door for support. Drunk and it was hardly the third hour of the day. Stephen wondered if Sir Geoff knew his bailiff had a habit of tapping the wine barrels this early in the morning. He wasn't about to trust his business to a drunken bailiff. "I've a question only he can answer," Stephen said shortly. "Since he's not here to answer it, I'll have to make do without."

Simon looked unconcerned. "Suit yourself. Shall I tell you called?"

"That won't be necessary. Good day."

Stephen went down the stairs, wondering what to do now. Sir Geoff probably would go on from Hereford to Winchester for the Michaelmas reporting of the county's accounts to the Exchequer. That meant there was a good chance he'd be gone for at least a month. Baynard might be willing to wait a month for his apprentice, but Stephen wasn't willing to wait that long for his shillings. Well, he thought, I'm really only a part time coroner. The rest of my time is my own.

As he rode out of the gate, it occurred to him that the Bromptone manor was not that far off — just beyond Ditton Priors, which was about ten miles to the north, up the Rea valley. There was a road a mile or so back that went north around the Clee and passed through Ditton Priors. He could be there by noon. With a short break for dinner and a few questions, he could be back in Ludlow by dark. With luck, the family would spill this apprentice's location. Breaking an apprentice contract was a serious matter, after all, and while crown officers don't usually take an interest in such matters, the family couldn't know why he was interested and they should cooperate with his inquiry. That would put him halfway to his quarry. The whole matter might even be concluded by the end of the week.

Smiling, he heeled the mare into her ground-eating trot. He hoped no one died an unnatural death while he was busy.

The one person who knows everyone about is the local vicar, and there's seldom a person who is more willing to talk to strangers than a vicar, as most country people will give a cold shoulder to a stranger. Vicars, who are very busy persons, are often not at home, but Stephen got lucky. He tracked down the vicar of Ditton Priors in his garden, where he was hoeing at the weeds strangling his late season cauliflower, under the watchful eye of a woman who was sitting on an upturned bucket with a leather tankard on her knee. That cauliflower looked overly ready for harvest in Stephen's opinion. But he had not come to chat about the state of the cauliflower, so he said nothing about it and got straight to his business, after the obligatory pleasantries. The vicar spat just like any other country person, since that was what he was, and said the Bromptones lived on the road to Middleton Priors, by the brook. You couldn't miss it: it was the biggest house this side of the bridge. And what, pray tell kind of business did he have with the Bromptones, if you don't mind the vicar's asking, as the family were his parishioners.

Stephen didn't feel like tarrying, but he did feel obliged to say something, since the vicar had been so quick and friendly with directions. "I've business with Peter Bromptone."

"Ah," the vicar nodded and took off his wool cap to mop his bald brow. "The younger son. What kind of business might that be?"

Stephen wasn't a particularly chatty person, but there was no harm in saying, "He's apprentice to a draper in Ludlow."

"I'd heard that. Yes, I had."

"And he's run away from his master."

"Oh, now that's news." The vicar frowned thoughtfully. He wiped his mouth. "Let me have some of that, Sally. I'm doing all the work and you're getting all the drink."

"If you'd switch places with me for a day, you'd know that was a lie," said Sally, a substantially built woman whose feet were bare and dirty, for most country folk did without shoes in good weather to save on the leather. But she passed the tankard, and the vicar took a swallow, his Adam's apple bobbing.

The vicar said generously, "Would you like some, your honor?"

"That's all right, thanks. What do you hear of him?"

The vicar opened his mouth to speak, but Sally beat him to it. "He got married. Although that seems odd. Apprentices aren't supposed to marry. Right?"

"That's right," Stephen said. "When did this happen?"

"Sometime last week," Sally said, slapping her knee. "Told you so, Tim. Told you he wasn't supposed to get married."

The vicar looked disgruntled. Stephen thought it was from Sally's rebuke until Sally added, "He's just mad because he wasn't invited to do the honors and didn't get no wedding fee. Why, none of us was even invited to the festivities."

"That's because there weren't no wedding feast," Tim the vicar said. "The young fool eloped. Got married without permission of his parents."

Stephen digested this information, wondering what sort of domestic stew he was about to find. He said, "Who was the bride?"

The vicar curled his brow as if in disapproval, but it was clear he was enjoying himself. "She wasn't from around here."

"She was a real pretty piece, I tell you," Sally chortled, stroking imaginary long hair with her fingertips. She added in a confiding voice. "I saw her when the boy came through on the way home to present her. There was quite a row over it, Benjamin said."

Stephen was confused. "Benjamin?"

"The Bromptones' blacksmith," Tim said. "He's here often. Sweet on a girl in the village."

"He'll get her with child but he won't marry her," Sally intoned. "He ain't the marrying kind. He's the diddling and run-away kind."

"I've warned her, but she won't listen," Tim said sadly. "Well, it's not a fit subject for discussion around this gentleman," Tim went on with exaggerated dignity. "I'm sure he has better things to do."

"Right," Sally said. Then she said shrewdly, "Your honor didn't really say what your business was with young Peter."

"I've a wedding present for him," Stephen said.

"Ha," Sally laughed. "That's rich."

Stephen shrugged. But then he thought better of treating these decent people so cavalierly. "I have been asked to find him."

"Why?" Sally and Tim said together.

"You can't just let apprentices run away," Stephen said. "He's got an obligation to fulfill."

"Right," Tim said. "An obligation. Matter of contract," he added knowingly.

There was a pause, as Sally and Tim pondered the majesty of the obligation of contracts, so Stephen saw an opportunity to get in an undisturbed word. "Peter might still be home, don't you think?"

"He might," Tim said, "though he didn't come to church on Sunday."

"He never came to church when he lived here," Sally said. "Except when his parents made him. Why should that change now? But he could still be there. Benjamin didn't say if he'd gone."

Stephen pondered that for a moment. Then a question popped into his head. "You don't happen to remember the girl's name, do you?"

"Amicia," Sally said. She drew out the name with a hiss. "That's what I heard."

"Thanks," Stephen said. He turned the mare toward the road north. "Good day to you."

"And you, sir," Sally and the vicar said together.

The last Stephen saw of them the vicar was reaching for the tankard. Sally pushed him away with a laugh.

Wickley, the Bromptone manor, was a prosperous looking stone house with a squat, round tower attached to one corner. Unlike Sir Geoff's house, the Bromptones' had no embankment or palisade. Only a low stone wall marked the manor grounds off from the thatch-roofed houses of its hamlet, which straggled along the road down to the river, where a mill wheel sonorously creaked away.

The yard here too was deserted and quiet. The stables were full, so Stephen tethered the mare at the door, put an oat bag on her, and crossed to the house, skirting a bull chained by his nose ring to a post at the foot of the steps. The bull eyed him with suspicion and then bent back to a little pile of hay beside the post.

The doors were open to let in the light and Stephen knew before he reached the top step from the commotion and clatter that he had arrived at the height of dinner.

His sudden appearance silhouetted in the doorway came as a surprise, for the clatter and clamor ceased abruptly, and all heads swiveled in his direction.

"Good morning," Stephen said as he slowly removed his riding gloves. "Please don't let me interrupt you."

"Well, whoever you are," said the big man seated in the high-backed chair before the fireplace, "come on in. Take a seat, stranger, and tell us what brings you to Wickley." He beckoned with a mallet of a hand toward an empty place at a bench on the right. A servant hurriedly left his place at the lower left-hand table to escort Stephen to the spot indicated.

Stephen let himself be led to the spot and sat down. A bowl of water and a towel were placed in front of him so he could wash his hands, and immediately afterward a trencher of sliced lamb on a slab of bread accompanied by a bowl of fish soup, by the aroma, appeared as if out of the ground.

The big man could only be Master Bromptone. He had brown hair only going slightly gray at the temples with flecks of gray streaking his neatly trimmed beard. His eyes were brown also, and revealed a lively intelligence as he surveyed his uninvited guest. His great shoulders strained at the rich green fabric of his coat, and his large fingered hands twirled a spoon.

To the left of Master Bromptone was a severe looking woman who must be his wife. On his right was an equally large and well-dressed man who favored a black coat with silver buttons, which went well with his black hair and beard and dark predatory eyes. On the right of the hawk-eyed man was a smaller version of Master Bromptone who looked too old to be an apprentice — an elder son, Stephen guessed. There were two girls of about twelve who took after the wife. The rest appeared to be servants, except for five hard men at Stephen's table who all wore black livery. The hawk-eyed man's companions? No one in the hall looked like Peter Bromptone and his new wife.

Everyone waited for Stephen to speak. He finished washing his hands and dried them on the towel, which he handed to the servant, who had remained at his elbow for this purpose.

"Well, good company," Stephen said, "my name is Stephen Attebrook. And you are Lord Bromptone?"

"I am Arnold Bromptone," the lord said, exchanging quick glances with his hawk-eyed companion, who was introduced as Nigel FitzSimmons.

Stephen expected Bromptone to give him another opportunity to state his business, and he readied an explanation.

But instead, it was FitzSimmons who spoke. "You are," FitzSimmons said with studied casualness, "related to the earl of the same name?"

"My cousin."

"Ah. Your brother wouldn't happen to be William Attebrook?"

For some reason the atmosphere at the head table had grown noticeably chiller, although Stephen could not understand why. "We have the fortune to have shared the same parents," he said.

"How remarkable."

"It usually is so with brothers. But that's all we share."

"You don't get along?"

"He disinherited me."

"Disinherited, are you," FitzSimmons said with amusement that Stephen found nettling.

Before Stephen could respond, Bromptone said with studied casualness, "Aren't you a crown officer? I heard something about you a few weeks ago."

Stephen was glad Bromptone had brought the conversation back to earth. He had no idea why FitzSimmons seemed so keen to needle him. He said, "I've taken service as Sir Geoffrey Randall's deputy."

"Right," Bromptone drawled. "That's it." Again, he and FitzSimmons exchanged quick glances. "Your work hasn't brought you this far north, has it? I hadn't heard that anyone had died here. And we're rather out of your jurisdiction here in Shropshire."

"I've different business. Not crown business, actually. I regret that it isn't more pleasant and that I have to trouble you with it. I've been requested to locate your son, Peter. There is, apparently, a matter of an unfinished apprentice contract."

Oddly, Bromptone looked puzzled for a moment. Then he relaxed, but just a trifle. FitzSimmons leaned over his trencher, elbows on the table, and rested his chin in his hands. His expression was sharp, his smile small and nasty.

"And who made this request?" Bromptone asked.

"Anselin Baynard."

"Oh," Bromptone said. "Him. That bastard. If he wants Peter, let that piece of scum come here himself."

Stephen was taken aback by Bromptone's venom. Peter's imbroglio was a mere financial matter, after all, and eventually would be dealt with like one, which could easily mean a friendly settlement that allowed Peter to walk away from the contract. Stephen looked at his nails and said, "Who's Peter's surety — you?"

Bromptone didn't speak, but his scowl answered for him.

Stephen went on: "You know what will happen if Peter's not returned. Baynard could sue for the surety. Or he could demand indenture. Either way, you'll have to hire lawyers. You'll be out the surety and what you paid the lawyers. And if it's indenture he wants . . ." Stephen shrugged. "A waste of money, paying lawyers."

"Let him sue. He'll never collect," Bromptone sneered. "And he'll never have my boy in indenture. He'll be dead before that happens." He and Fitzsimmons exchanged glances again.

"Where has Peter gone, by the way?"

"I'm damned if I'll tell you," Bromptone said.

Stephen wiped his mouth with his napkin and stood up. It was rude to go on eating after what had been said. "As I feared, I've brought you unpleasantness. I'll go, then, and take my bad business with me, and leave you in peace. The lamb was excellent, and so was the soup. My compliments on your kitchen, Lord Bromptone. Madame Bromptone."

He bowed, stepped over his bench, and strode quickly toward the front doors, trying hard not to limp.

Stephen was less than half a mile south of Ditton Priors when he heard the horses approaching from behind. At first, he thought it was a post rider, although this was not a post road. He cocked an ear, and decided that, no, it was two horses, not just one. He turned behind to see what this was all about. Round the bend, the two horses and riders appeared at full gallop.

The riders drew their swords at the sight of him.

He recognized them. They were two of the five soldiers at his table at Bromptone House.

They were coming straight for him.

They meant to kill him.

Whatever for?

These thoughts raced through his mind as he sat paralyzed with surprise.

But then training and experience took over.

He gave the mare his heels and laid across her neck.

She was a good galloper, but the pursuers had the jump. The mare had barely gathered her hooves to run when they were beside him, one man on either flank.

Stephen sensed more than saw the flash of the swords as they descended, like a pair of scythes shearing wheat.

Another man would have been cut in half by those massive strokes, but Stephen knew a Moorish trick that could buy him just a few moments. He threw himself to the left, so that he hung from the mare's side, an arm around her neck and his right leg hooking the cantle of his saddle.

One sword sang in the air above him. The other thudded into the cantle, nearly taking his leg off, and the sword stuck in the wood of the cantle. The soldier, a young man just out of boyhood, struggled to pull it free from the wood of the saddle.

Stephen grasped the soldier's arm and let go of the mare.

His weight pulled the soldier with him to the ground.

Because Stephen knew what was coming, he rolled with the impact, though it was stunning and knocked some of the wind out of him.

The soldier was caught by surprise, landed with a terrific thud, and didn't move. The mare and the soldier's now riderless horse raced up the road and disappeared around the next bend.

The soldier's sword had come loose and lay a short distance away in the road. Stephen rose to fetch it, but the other soldier wheeled his horse and charged.

The other soldier came on, leaning forward and giving point. Stephen had seen this before. The point was a diversion. The death blow would be a back-handed cut with a twirl of the wrist.

To turn and run was certain death.

He drew his dagger from the small of his back and waited for his moment.

At the last instant, he threw himself across the horse's path, out of reach of the sword. He rolled to his feet and stood up.

The soldier was already turning the horse again. He was an excellent rider and it was a well trained, responsive animal that knew its business. They had clearly performed as a team before in this kind of work.

Stephen edged toward the sword lying in the road. The older soldier didn't try to charge this time. He urged his horse after Stephen and tried to hack him down from above.

Stephen dodged this way and that, hoping the soldier would over commit on a slash, which might allow him to close and wrestle. The soldier was too cautious and experienced to make that kind of mistake. Instead, he jostled Stephen gradually toward the edge of the road and the enclosing wood that bordered it. Who knew what obstacles lay back there? Stephen had had a friend who'd been killed during a duel when he'd back-peddled into a pile of manure and fallen.

As he stepped onto the verge of the road, he saw his moment.

When the soldier raised his sword for another cut, Stephen dashed forward and to his right, seizing the bridle. He ran so sharply and forcefully that his momentum caught the horse by surprise and pulled it off balance. The animal's neck bent and turned. There was a moment's hesitation when Stephen thought he had failed.

The horse toppled onto its side.

Stephen ran around to get at the soldier before he had a chance to stand as the horse regained its feet, leaving its rider on the ground. The soldier hacked at Stephen to keep him away and stood up.

He was between Stephen and the other sword. Heaving to catch his breath, Stephen debated again whether to run, but with his bad foot he doubted he could out run the soldier. The soldier smiled. It did nothing to make his features more attractive. His nose had been flattened and he had survived a horrible sword cut to his jaw that left his face looking caved in. He moved with deceptive smoothness. Some big men were slow, but Stephen was willing to bet he was quick on his feet. The soldier edged closer, sword at his ear in the guard of wrath. The soldier saw the dagger and was cautious. He must know that a man with a dagger presented some danger to him. But you could not fight a cautious swordsman with just a dagger.

Stephen turned and ran.

The soldier ran after him.

Stephen heard the pounding feet behind him and knew he was right: he couldn't out run the soldier.

He pretended to stumble.

The soldier raised the sword high above his head. It hung there for what seemed a terribly long moment, then came its swishing descent at Stephen's head — a blow that could part his skull to the collarbone like a melon.

Stephen stepped into and under the blow. He held the dagger in the high shield, with one hand near the tip of the blade and the other on the grip. The force of the blow on the dagger blade jolted his wrists as he deflected the cut to the side, then he stabbed the soldier in the throat. The point of the foot-long dagger blade penetrated effortlessly, as if into a pudding, and emerged from the back of the soldier's neck at the base of his skull. The soldier looked startled and stuck out his tongue. The light in his eyes rapidly faded. He toppled over backward, dead before he hit the ground.

Stephen bent and wiped the dagger on the dead man's coat.

He staggered over to see about the other soldier.

The fellow was still alive. His eyes fluttered open when Stephen patted his cheeks. Then the eyes focused on Stephen.

Stephen put his dagger point under the man's chin. "Who put you up to this?" he demanded. "Bromptone? FitzSimmons?"

The soldier only grimaced.

Stephen was on the verge of losing his temper. He pricked hard. "Who! Why!"

"You bastard . . ." the man gasped in a barely audible voice. ". . . rot in hell . . ."

The wind hissed out of the man. He didn't breathe again. His face went waxy, a sight Stephen knew only too well.

Stephen stood up and sheathed the dagger. He ached all over from the fall. His bad foot throbbed so badly he could barely stand on it. His palms hurt from the impact of the sword.

The road was tranquil and still. The wind stirred the branches overhead. A robin flitted across the road into the bushes, a streak of red, white and brown. Other birds were singing. He heard the buzzing of a wasp. The golden greens and browns around him seemed brighter and more clear than normal. He took a deep breath and let it out. The air was sweet. He was still alive, when he had no right to be. He wondered why some who did not deserve to had to die, while the less deserving went on living.

Presently, he dragged the bodies into the woods and went looking for his horse.

Chapter 5

Gilbert smoothed the fabric of the shirt on the table top and leaned back to inspect the little rent and the crusted circle at arm's length, not easy in the light of a single candle guttering on the table of the deserted hall.

"Can't see as well as I used to," he muttered. "Getting harder to write too."

"Poor dear," Edith said. "You're getting old."

"Not too old to give you a good romp, my dear," Gilbert said.

"But not as often," she said.

"Hush, woman. I'm as fit as any stallion." Gilbert's finger ran around the little slit. He poked a forefinger through it. "Seems we were remiss," he said to Stephen.

"I was remiss."

"Don't be so hard on yourself."

"I should have had him stripped."

"It would have been unseemly there on the roadside. And there were women present."

"Still . . ."

"Still nothing. Don't blame yourself, I say. You've found it out. That's all that matters." He stroked his lower lip. "I'll have to amend the report. We'll have to interview this parish priest, and you'll have to see the wound for yourself, I imagine. That's proper form, regrettably. Don't worry about the details. I'll have the body disinterred. You can come round and view it when it's done. Come now," he said at the look on Stephen's face. "He'll only have been dead four days. It won't be so bad. Just don't eat first."

"I'll be sure not to." Boot and sock off, Stephen rubbed his bad foot. Gilbert and Edith politely pretended not to notice the stump.

"Good lad." Gilbert continued to stroke his lower lip. "What really concerns me is this attempt on your life. I've never heard of this FitzSimmons character, but I know a bit of this Bromptone. He went over to the barons earlier this year. Odd that Bromptone should want you killed over such a trivial thing as an apprentice's contract."

"But it wasn't Bromptone's men. I'm sure the two were Fitzsimmons'."

"Perhaps this Fitzsimmons wanted to do his friend a favor."

"A costly favor."

"So it has turned out." Gilbert's eyes narrowed. "No, it couldn't be the contract business. I know you say Bromptone was full of hatred for Baynard, but it's got to be more than that to provoke murder."

"What then?" Stephen asked. He put his boot back on.

Gilbert thought aloud. "The majority of this county are for the king. But there are a sizeable minority who support the barons. And there have been incidents between the two factions. Not open war — a few beatings of the barons' supporters, an odd fire, a killing or two of some prominent baron's man, a man thrown into prison here and there. Since the king returned to power, his folk have been feeling their strength. It could be the barons' people are planning something in reply, and there you show up, a king's officer acting on Baynard's behalf — one of the town's loudest partisans for the king. Could be, they're afraid you have your nose to the ground about whatever they're cooking up. So right or not, they have marked you down. I'd say, you'd better watch your back from now on."

"I'll hire Harry as a bodyguard. He could use honest work."

Gilbert changed subjects. "What did you do with those two fellows?"

"Pulled them into the forest, and sent their horses on their way."

Edith regarded Stephen over the top of her ale tankard. "A coroner could lose his job leaving bodies lying around like that."

"Not to mention his head," Gilbert said. "But with luck, FitzSimmons and Bromptone won't know you're still alive for some days yet."

"But he'll wonder when his men don't come back," Edith said.

"That he will. That he will."

"I wonder what they have planned," Stephen said.

"At worst, it could be is another rising. Perhaps Montfort is planning to come back."

"I'd like to meet this Montfort."

Gilbert smiled thinly. "Don't say that too loud round here. Even with the place empty someone's bound to hear and report you. And don't even think you'll get away with sitting on the fence. There's no patience with fence sitters these days."

The next morning, Gilbert sent a boy from Ludford to let Stephen know it was time. He rode without eagerness across the Teme and up the slope to the parish church, which stood in a little square at the top of the rise. He rather expected Gilbert to have laid the body beside the grave. But no one was by the pile of freshly turned earth in the graveyard. The boy motioned him toward the church. "They're in there, sir," he said. "Waiting for you."

Stephen went in, leaving the boy to linger in the doorway to watch.

The smell of decay was strong, over-powering the musty aroma of old straw and dankness that always seemed to fill little stone churches like this.

The fact Gilbert had chosen to bring the body in didn't seem to sit well with the vicar Hamo, who looked distinctly distressed. The two workmen who had dug up the coffin and carried it inside stood nearby.

Gilbert turned to him. "Ah," he said, "you've arrived."

"Let's get on with it," Stephen said, his throat constricted.

Gilbert gave Stephen a rag soaked with sour wine. He tied a wine-soaked rag of his own over his nose and mouth. Stephen did the same.

"A moment, my son," Gilbert said through the rag, his words muffled. "We'll say a prayer for him first."

Stephen expected the vicar to lead it, but Gilbert didn't wait for him. Instead, hands folded and head bowed, looking oddly more priestlike than the vicar, Gilbert launched straight into mumbled Latin. Stephen bowed his head but clasped his hands behind his back. Gilbert paused. He shot a glance at Stephen, then kicked him in the leg.

"You may have abandoned Him, but He hasn't abandoned you," Gilbert said sharply. "I, more than anyone, should know about such things. Come on, now!"

Not wishing an argument, Stephen pressed his hands together.

Gilbert finished and looked up. "Well, then, that's better, isn't it? I suppose we should get to work."

The vicar went back to looking distressed.

The two workmen leaned forward so they would be sure not to miss anything. It seemed there was entertainment value to be derived from a sight others regarded as gruesome and unpleasant.

This irritated Stephen. Death stripped every man of his dignity, and to be dug up after burial, to suffer exposure to public view the corruption which inevitably followed death, was too much an added humiliation. Patrick probably hadn't had much dignity in life, but he didn't deserve such humiliation in death.

"You three," he said to the vicar and the workmen, "you can go. We'll manage here alone, if you please."

The vicar looked relieved but the workmen seemed ready to argue.

"Now!" Stephen barked.

The workmen jerked at the tone of command, and reluctantly turned toward the door, followed closely by the vicar.

"And you there," Stephen said to the boy. "Out and close that door."

"Right, sir," the boy peeped.

"You've sent away our help," Gilbert said, when they had gone.

"You know how to pry out a nail, don't you?"

"Well, yes."

"Then let's get this done. I can scarcely breathe."

"He is a bit ripe now."

"You'd be too after four days."

Gilbert attacked the coffin lid with one of the pry bars. The nails screeched as they came free. He pulled off the lid and set it aside. Patrick lay inside sewn into his linen burial shroud, the outlines of his face visible. But corruption had swollen the body so that Patrick's arms strained at the fabric as if reaching out for something.

"We'll have to lift him out," Gilbert said. He moved to Patrick's head. "Come on. You'll have to help me. I can't do it myself."

The notion of touching the dead man made Stephen's skin crawl, as if death could be transmitted by touch. He suppressed a shudder, though, and moved to Patrick's feet. Together they lifted Patrick out of the coffin and placed him on the ground.

Although the windows were open, it was dim in the church.

"We'll need a light," Stephen said.

"Good idea."

Stephen lit three votive candles at the rack by the door and set them on the coffin.

"Mind you don't knock one of them over," Gilbert said. "We don't want a fire."

"And roast poor Paddy? I'll try to be careful."

Gilbert slit the shroud from head to foot and folded it back. Free from their linen restraints, Patrick's arms sprang up as if to embrace Gilbert. Patrick had been dressed in what looked like his best clothes: a blue coat, a white linen shirt and green stockings, but no shoes. Decay made the body appear monstrously fat, and it strained at the clothing as if to burst out of them. The face was swollen and puffy, skin mottled with black patches, the mouth a gaping O displaying yellow teeth, a hideous grimace caught in mid-moan.

"You'll have to cut him out of his clothes," Stephen said.

"I suppose." Gilbert sighed. He went to work with his knife on Patrick's coat. He began to hum a saucy little tune, something called The Merry Widow. "Hope his wife doesn't find out we've done this. She'll be upset that we've cut up his best suit."

"I won't tell her Paddy's going to arrive in heaven bareassed if you don't."

"Just keep an eye on those windows, so somebody else doesn't have the chance to do the same," Gilbert said.

Stephen strolled over and peered out each window. At one he caught the workmen lurking. "Get away from there!" he shouted, and the workmen scurried away.

He turned back to Gilbert. "Should have charged admission."

"How stupid of us. We're just not thinking."

"That's why I'm so poor."

"You just haven't married right," Gilbert said. "That's the trick. You'll have to ask your cousin to find you a proper rich wife."

"It's a little late for that," Stephen muttered.

"What?"

"Never mind."

Gilbert sat back on his heels. "There. That should do it."

He reached for one of the candles and bent over to inspect Patrick's chest.

"There it is," Gilbert said. He pointed to a barely visible slit of a wound about an inch wide on the left side below the heart. "Into the lung, I'd say."

"And the heart?"

"Can't tell just from looking. We'll have to probe it — and measure."

Stephen's stomach roiled.

"I'll get it," Gilbert said. He had a short measuring stick with the inches marked off in blue paint. He wormed the stick into the wound as far as it would go, then pulled it out and held it up to the light. "Three inches, I'd say. Don't think it hit the heart. The angle's wrong." He indicated that the penetration went diagonally into the chest rather than straight in. "Like someone thrusting at him slightly from the side, aiming for the heart, but landing a trifle wide and low."

He simulated a dagger blow with his right hand against Stephen's chest.

"He probably didn't die right away from a wound like that, then," Stephen said.

"No, he could have walked some distance before he collapsed. That tallies with your observations — no other tracks but his at the ditch."

"In the village?"

"Most likely."

"But nobody saw or heard anything."

"So, they said."

For good measure, Gilbert turned Patrick over. He and Stephen inspected every inch of his skin, but saw no other wounds. They put Patrick back on his linen shroud.

Gilbert stood up. "There should be a bowl of water around here somewhere. And some soap."

"I see it." Stephen brought the bowl and cake over, and they took turns washing their hands, and then Gilbert cleaned off the little measuring stick.

"Who's going to sew him up?" Gilbert asked.

"You don't expect me to do it," Stephen said.

"Well, I cut his clothes off. I'd think it was your turn."

"My turn! You're the clerk."

"Pulling rank, are you?"

"Damned right. Besides, I'd just make a mess of it. Stab myself. Maybe even stab you."

Gilbert knelt back down. "Where's Edith when I need her? She's handier with a needle and thread than I am."

"I can imagine what she'll say when I fetch her for you," Stephen said dryly.

"Ah, no, let's not do that. I get enough of her sharp tongue as it is," Gilbert said.

In about a quarter hour, Gilbert had Patrick crudely stitched back into his shroud. He tossed the remains of Patrick's clothes into the coffin. "Time to box him up and replant him."

They lifted the body into the coffin and replaced the lid.

Stephen opened the church door with a jerk and found the boy crouching at the crack. The boy scuttled back, looking fearful. Stephen passed him and called for the workmen, who were skulking in the graveyard.

The workmen renailed the lid and carried the coffin back to its grave.

Stephen and Gilbert followed them into the morning sunlight.

Gilbert gazed at his hands. "I could use another scrubbing."

"A bath would be more like it," Stephen said. He felt soiled.

"Not a bad idea. You paying?"

Stephen felt generous after making Gilbert sew up the shroud. He said, "Least I can do for a grave robber."

"Speak for yourself."

Chapter 6

The Wobbly Kettle had the ill luck to be across the street from St. John's Hospital. A prime service of bathhouses was prostitution, and this put the place at odds with the hospital when a particularly strict abbot took over. The prior preached a sermon against prostitutes one Sunday and, at his urging, the friars pelted the front of the house with gobs of mud. Certain employees of the Kettle paraded before the hospital and, when the friars came to the windows to condemn the commotion, they uplifted their skirts to show the friars what they were missing due to their lives of contemplation and denial. A fight broke out in the street between whores and friars, with the friars getting the worst of it. Eventually, the parties reached a settlement that provided that the ladies of the house would not solicit business on the street in view of the hospital, nor service its patients or churchmen.

"Doesn't that include you, then?" Stephen asked innocently as they reached the door.

"No," Gilbert said. "I'm in minor orders now. Doesn't count." He pointed to the top of his bald head. "See that? God made me that way, not some friar's razor."

It was a slow day and an attendant escorted them straight to the rear of the house, where the baths were in a large shed-like room with eight round tubs, four in a row on a side and separated from each other by curtains on which hunting and fishing scenes were embroidered. Most of the curtains were drawn, so Stephen could not see who occupied the tubs within as he made his way back to a tub that was free.

The attendant drew the curtain for Stephen and left. Steam rose from the surface of the water. Stephen tested it with a finger. It was hot to the touch and when he climbed in and sank to his chin, he gasped with the impact of the heat. A servant entered with a cup of wine. He put the cup on a board that lay across one side of the barrel-like tub.

Stephen sipped the wine, feeling as though he could melt in the heat.

Presently a girl came in. She held a round, rough looking sponge and a cake of brown soap. "I'm Kate," she said. "I'll scrub you for a halfpenny."

Stephen grinned. "All right." A halfpenny was pretty steep for a scrubbing, but having received his shillings only yesterday from Baynard, he felt almost rich.

Kate unbuttoned the front of her dress and slipped out of it. She was naked underneath, and thin, as if she didn't get enough to eat. She had small breasts and a narrow waist. Stephen couldn't help staring at her.

Kate climbed in the tub and settled behind him, straddling his body with her legs. Her thighs, where they brushed against his body, were silky, and her breasts, which pressed lightly into his back, felt soft and delicious. He wanted to turn around and grab her, but instead he closed his eyes and hung his head. She soaped his shoulders, wet his hair, and soaped that too. She applied the sponge, which was scratchy, but she had been doing this enough not to use it too hard. Then she kneaded his head and shoulders with surprisingly strong fingers as if he was a lump of dough. Stephen sighed deeply. She rinsed him off with another pitcher that had hung out of sight on a hook on the side of the tub.

"Would you like the full services of the house?" Kate asked.

Stephen nodded. Kate shifted around so that she straddled him on his lap. "Don't be so tense," she said. "Relax. It won't take long. Never does."

"All better now?" Kate asked when they finished, and she climbed out of the tub.

Stephen felt like sinking beneath the water. He didn't care if he drowned.

Kate found a towel on the sideboard and dried herself off. She slid back into her dress. "Got your pennies, love?" she asked.

Stephen waved at his clothes, which hung on a peg. She opened his purse and counted three half pennies for herself.

"Bye now," she said, parting the curtain.

"You're a true artist," he managed to say.

"I don't mind going all out for a handsome one like you," she said.

Stephen wondered if she'd say that if she had seen his stump.

She turned away and was gone.

Only then did Stephen realize that she'd got as much as a workman earned in almost two full work days. He'd spent more than four times what he had intended when he entered the Kettle. Yet, he couldn't complain that he'd been robbed.

The water had grown tepid. Stephen climbed out, got dressed and returned to the front of the house. Gilbert had not finished, so he bought a pitcher of wine and settled onto a bench to wait. He heard voices in the hall and, thinking it was Gilbert, he poured another cup. Instead, Clement, Baynard's bailiff, emerged from the tub room. Still feeling lightheaded, Stephen waved him to take a seat.

"Do you need a refill?" he asked Clement.

"That would be nice," Clement said. He extended his cup and Stephen filled it.

They didn't have much to say to each other, so they sat in silence for a while, until Clement burst out, "Fine weather we're having, after that storm."

"Yes." Stephen sipped his wine.

"Heard you were up in Ludford this morning. Any trouble up there?"

"No, it was old trouble."

"What old trouble, if you don't mind my asking."

Stephen didn't feel like talking, but he said, "It was about Patrick Carter's death. Seems it wasn't an accident after all."

Clement looked startled. "Really."

"Yes. Someone slipped a knife in him." He paused and added, "Missed the wound the first time around."

"How can you be certain?"

"We dug him up."

Clement regarded Stephen as if he had gone mad. "You don't say. That's a bit unusual, isn't it?"

"Very. But, duty, you know. Unpleasant chore." Stephen wrinkled his nose at the memory.

Clement drank and asked, "Any idea who did it?"

Stephen shook his head. "Nobody seems to know anything. Have you heard anything?"

"Oh, no." Clement paused. "Might've been robbery, you know. Patrick may have looked the poor carter but he always had money about him. Not much, mind you, but enough to tempt the desperate."

"That's been suggested. But no money was taken. He had two half pennies in his purse when we found him."

"Ah. Maybe someone scared them off."

"Could be."

"You don't think so?" Clement studied a girl descending the stairs. She raised her eyebrows in a question and he shook his head.

"I don't know what to think. All I know is, I've a murdered man on my hands, and no idea how or why he died."

"That must be frustrating. It isn't often you don't know who's done murder. What are you going to do?"

"I suppose I'll have to make inquiries until I learn something."

Clement rubbed a water stain on the table. "What led you to suspect murder?"

Stephen told him about his meeting with Molly, Patrick's widow.

Clement swirled the wine in his cup. "Got to be going," he said abruptly.

Then he fumbled in his belt pouch. His fist emerged clutching a rolled parchment, which was sealed with wax and a ribbon. "I forgot. I'm supposed to give you this." He held it out. "A writ of attachment for debt. Master Baynard asked me to have you serve it when you find Peter."

Stephen prodded the roll with a fingertip. The writ would allow Peter's arrest. Serving it was not part of their arrangement — ordinarily, there was a separate fee for that. "I was not engaged to serve writs. I was engaged to find someone. How you get him back is your affair."

Clement's mouth worked. "That's not our understanding."

"Well, it's mine. Your master asked to find the boy, and found is what you'll get."

Clement's anger gave way to calculation and perhaps a trace of contempt. "So," he said, "you'll want extra money."

Stephen was beginning to feel soiled. He didn't want the trouble entailed in capturing and forcibly returning Peter when he was found. If anything, Stephen's sympathies lay with the lost apprentice. But he hated to admit to himself that he wanted the money, although it put off the prospect of ruin just a little bit further.

"How much?" Clement grated.

"Another six shillings."

"Done."

Stephen was surprised Clement agreed so easily, and with his master's money, too.

Stephen asked, "Did you know Peter?"

"Certainly. I know all the apprentices."

"You knew, of course, that Peter had married?"

Clement said, "I heard that."

"You knew the girl also?"

"It was hard to miss her when she came around." Clement grinned salaciously. "They were like a pair of doves."

"Who was she?"

Clement shrugged. "Some girl from Gloucester."

"How is it he was able to marry a girl from Gloucester? Did he often get down there?"

"No, of course not," Clement said. "They met here and there, bundling in alleys and orchards, that sort of thing." At Stephen's puzzled look, Clement added, "She was a maid to Lucy Wattepas."

"I'm sorry. I'm new here. I've heard the name, but its significance escapes me."

"Wattepas — Leofwine Wattepas, alderman of the Palmer's Guild," Clement said impatiently. "She's his wife."

Stephen was familiar enough with the institutions of the town to understand the significance of that. The Palmer's Guild was an association of wealthy merchants whose purpose was to fund the salaries of chaplains at various charities and to provide for a program of insurance for its members. It was almost as important and powerful as the council of twelve, which actually ran the town. "And she ran off, too. How embarrassing that must be for Master Baynard, to lose an apprentice and to cause such an important family to lose a maid."

"Oh, it caused quite a falling out. It's got so neither of the masters will speak to the other, each blaming the other. It won't last, though. They bowl on the same team." He laughed and said, "You should see them at bowls, huffing around and pretending the other isn't there." More soberly he went on, "It's only on account of Mistress Wattepas that there's bad feeling. She'd be affronted if there wasn't, and you don't want to affront Mistress Wattepas."

"A formidable lady."

"You take that right."

"A little more wine, Master Clement?" Stephen asked. He offered the pitcher. Drinking with servants was not something he had been brought up to encourage, but he had long ago got used to drinking with soldiers and, now that it had occurred to Stephen that Clement could be helpful, the courtesy might loosen his tongue.

"Why, thank you." Clement poured, took a hearty swig and smacked his lips. "They've such good wine here."

"This Peter, you haven't told me what did he looks like."

"Oh, a handsome lad, at least that's what everyone said."

"You didn't think so."

Clement shrugged. "He was well enough set up — dark brown hair the color of good dirt, eyes the same. A fair complexion, but marred by freckles across his nose. A little taller than me, but slightly built and not much for fighting. He should be though, the way he talks. Sassed me when he first came, and I had to teach him his place." Clement clenched his fist at the memory. "He has trouble learning his lessons. He'd talk back to the king. Never shy about speaking his mind, that one."

"I would guess then that Peter and Master Baynard didn't get along."

Clement's eyes narrowed as if he was debating whether to answer. "Not well at all. They argued a lot."

"What about?"

"About anything that came into Peter's head. But often it was politics, although what Peter's business is with the running of the country, I don't know."

"Peter was for Montfort."

"Yes," Clement said. "When his family went over to the barons, Peter went with them, and wasn't silent about it. When the king came back to power, Peter still couldn't keep silent about it. It drove the master mad. He made Peter sleep in the barn and do chores. Pete took that hard. 'Prentices aren't supposed to do chores, you know."

"Yes, I was an apprentice once."

"You were? At what?"

Stephen ignored the question. He didn't want to talk about that unfortunate time of his life, especially with someone like Clement. "What about this debt?"

"What debt?"

"The one that Peter owes."

"Ah, the fool boy left a half wagon load of cloth out in the rain when he ran. It mildewed. He owes for the damage."

"How clumsy. More wine?"

"Don't mind if I do."

"Your visitor, my lady, the deputy coroner," the servant said. He drew back a few steps and turned about with precision more often seen in the court of an earl than the hall of a merchant, and marched away.

Mistress Lucy Wattepas put down her stylus and regarded Stephen. Her expression attempted to be noncommittal, but Stephen saw the calculation behind her chilly eyes, which traveled from his battered boots to his face. And he could guess what lay behind that measuring gaze. She wasn't sure how to treat him. There were many rungs on the social ladder, and the players' standing on those rungs in relation to another dictated how they played the game of society.

Her indecision arose from the fact that she wasn't, by rights, a lady. That title belonged to a woman of the gentry, not a merchant's wife. Yet she had pretensions, which were evident not only in the servant's manner of address and his behavior, but in her appearance and bearing. She wore a heavy chain of twisted gold. Her gown was an embroidered maroon, the sort of thing you'd expect to see on a gentry woman rather than a merchant's wife. Stephen guessed she was a gentry woman who had married down, which was not unusual in families having a surplus of daughters, and she had aspirations to reclaim her former place in society. Many merchants grew rich enough to buy themselves a manor and rise socially. Clearly, that had not happened yet for Mistress Wattepas. Stephen expected this was a source of discontent.

She, on the other hand, was having difficulty placing him. She knew that he was gentry, but poor. Poverty did not immediately eject one from the gentry but it could diminish one's standing. How much depended on connections. So there was Stephen's family to consider and whom he might know.

"A pleasure, sir," she said, making a claim to high standing by speaking in French, a language that many gentry far from London did not speak well. As the language of court, they were expected to know it unless they stood so far down the ladder that they were little better than yeomen. "May I offer you some refreshment?"

"No, thank you, my lady," Stephen said in court French, his pronunciation more correct than hers, and making the point that he accepted her gentry status but that he stood higher than she did.

Her mouth twisted, perhaps in a smile, at the message. She said, "How may I help you, sir?"

"My apologies, for the interruption," Stephen said. "I know you are busy. I do not require but a few moments of your valuable time. I ask only a favor."

"I am happy to do whatever is within my power," she said. Her lips pursed as if she was weighing how much any favor would put him in her debt.

"I am trying to locate someone," Stephen said.

Mistress Wattepas steepled her fingers. "This is not an official inquiry?"

"No. It is private business."

"Of yours?"

"Of a friend."

"What friend, if you don't mind my asking?"

Stephen hesitated. If she disliked Baynard it was not politic to mention him. So Stephen uttered the first name that popped into his head: "Gilbert Wistwode." He was immediately sorry. It made the task seem unimportant from Mistress Wattepas' perspective and rendered her less likely to be helpful.

"Poor Master Wistwode," she said in a way intended to be sympathetic but which could not help being disdainful. "Has he lost a servant girl?"

"He is owed a debt," Stephen said, regretting his mistake. He attempted to improvise by making the problem seem his. "I have taken it upon myself as his friend to speak to the debtor in hopes he will pay it."

"Ah," Mistress Wattepas said. Her fingers tapped the parchments before her.

"I don't know how I can possibly help you," she said. As she settled back in her chair, her elbow brushed a cylinder of copper, which clattered to the floor.

Stephen retrieved the cylinder. As he returned it to the table, he noticed that it was a seal in the form of a scales with a sword as the central balance — an odd seal for a merchant. He put the seal on the documents. Although they were upside down, they were written in so neat a hand that Stephen could see they consisted of ledgers of account and a few business letters.

He said, "Well, the young fellow seems to have disappeared."

"Young fellow?"

"Yes, an apprentice named Peter Bromptone."

"What could Master Wistwode possibly want with that silly boy."

"He ran up a bill and then disappeared."

"Have you inquired of his family?"

"They were not helpful."

Mistress Wattepas' mouth turned down in disapproval. "Of course. They are for Montfort, that despicable man. They have no honor."

"I understand that you may have a grievance against him yourself involving a maid."

"I have forgiven it."

Stephen was certain she had not. But he said, "That is generous of you."

"She is silly girl of no consequence. There is no point in becoming agitated over her."

"What is her name . . . Amicia . . . something."

"Canterbrigge. Amicia Canterbrigge," Mistress Wattepas said with difficulty as if the name itself hurt her tongue.

"And she came recommended to you?"

Mistress Wattepas waved a hand. "What does this have to do with that unpardonable little man?"

"She wed young Bromptone."

"Did she." Her tone suggested that this was news, but not unexpected. "Where did you learn that?"

"From a good source."

"His family?"

"Yes," Stephen lied.

"They would know."

"Without his father's permission."

She chuckled as she savored that revelation, for coming from the gentry she could appreciate its implications. "That boy should be whipped. What cheek."

"She came from a good family, then?"

"Who?"

"The girl, Amicia. I cannot imagine that a lady such as yourself would take into your household anyone but from a good family."

"They are," Mistress Wattepas grated. "Or were, until this. She has brought them down. The boy will never amount to anything. And she is an only daughter. Their spawn will inhabit the gutter," she said as if she relished the thought.

"And the girl left no word with anyone where she could be reached?"

"Of course not. The idea is preposterous. She's as much a runaway as he is."

"Ah. Certainly. And you said her father's name was . . . what?"

"I don't believe I spoke of her father."

"Perhaps you didn't. I thought you had. Who was he?"

"Just a draper."

"You dislike drapers?"

"Some drapers. Are you quite through? This is distracting."

"I do not mean to distress you."

"These matters are irksome."

"I beg your pardon, madam. In any case, you've been most helpful."

She was still shaking her head in bewilderment about how she could have been of assistance as he left the hall.

Chapter 7

Harry was at the Lower Broad Street gate when Stephen rode out of town Monday morning. The passage was blocked by a woman, a boy, and a flock of geese they were driving into town. Stephen couldn't get through immediately because the warden on duty was having trouble counting the flock in order to assess the toll. The geese kept milling around so that the warden, never good with figures in the first place, kept losing count and had to start over.

Harry eyed the geese with hungry eyes. "Here, here," he coaxed, holding out a scrap of bread. "I've got something for you."

"Keep those hands where they can be seen, Harry," Stephen said.

"Bugger off, your honor. Who says I can't give some poor starving geese a little charity?"

"I don't think it's charity you have in mind. Besides, their owner has her eyes on you."

"People always suspect the worst, grumpy bastards." He popped the crust in his mouth, however, and raised his begging bowl. "Care to make a donation, governor?"

Stephen dismounted and dropped to one knee beside Harry. "Do you have it?"

"What do you take me for? I'm an honest man. I told you I would be no party to fraud or forgery."

The warden threw them a look, and Stephen said, "Keep your voice down."

He had thought they'd made a deal and he was surprised with Harry's sudden attack of scruples. He started to straighten up, but Harry caught his wrist. Stephen had never felt the man's strength before and it was like being clasped in irons.

Harry said, "Aren't you going to leave me nothing? Rich fellow like you?"

He rattled the bowl and, when Stephen looked down, he saw a stick as wide around as the Wattepas' seal had somehow appeared there among the few coins Harry had collected that morning.

Stephen dropped a penny in the bowl and palmed the stick. A glance at the end showed an excellent replica of the drawing of the seal he had left with Harry yesterday.

"That good enough for you?" Harry asked.

"With skills like that, Harry, you could be a rich man yourself."

"They hang forgers you know."

"I'll be your partner. No one but me has to know you're the source."

"You'd break under torture."

The warden had started his count over again, so Stephen said to Harry to make conversation, "It's awfully smoky today."

"There was a fire last night in Ludford. One of the mills burned down. You didn't hear the commotion?"

"No."

"And you call yourself a soldier. Bet the Moors could've ridden right through your camp while you slept. Yeah, it was a big fire. Lit up the sky like a bonfire. And all the shouting! You could hear it from the Shield."

"Sorry I missed it."

"Wish I could go see. You wouldn't consider giving me a ride over, would you?"

"Sorry, Harry. I'm headed to Gloucester today and it's a long ride."

"Gloucester, is it? Never been there. Always wanted to go. Doesn't look like I'll get there now. They say it's a fair town."

"It's all right. A lot like Ludlow, only bigger. You're not missing anything."

The warden finally had finished his count. The woman paid up, and the boy snapped his switch to drive the flock up the street. Stephen flicked a farthing at Harry. "For the news," he said.

"You're too kind, governor."

"Just remember to come in out of the rain, Harry."

Stephen mounted the mare and rode through the gate.

Across the Teme, the road forked. The main road continued up the slope to the village proper; another road turned left and ran along the riverbank, while yet a third wended westward. Stephen went left. A fulling mill lay in that direction only a short distance away, its water wheel creaking under the current of the mill race. There was another mill beyond it which Stephen could not see. This must be the one that burned, for a pall of thin smoke was rising from that direction. One of the mills belonged to Ancelin Baynard. Stephen shivered with a premonition. He turned left.

A short way down the road, a pair of huge oaks stood athwart the river road, their branches arching overhead and entwining, creating the impression of an enormous gate. Stephen passed through and saw the ruined mill. Only a pile of smoldering timbers remained. A crowd of young boys lined the fence, while within the enclosure a dozen workers, who had nothing to do, sat under beeches whose remaining leaves were singed by the fire.

Anselin Baynard stood before the pile. The stench from the fire and the still rising smoke made the air practically unbreathable. Having had his view, Stephen thought about riding on, but Baynard turned and spotted him.

Baynard looked as though he wanted to avoid conversation as much as Stephen did, but since they had seen each other, it would have been too uncivil to pretend they hadn't.

They came together at the fence. "Your mill?" Stephen said.

"I dare say," Baynard spat.

"A great loss. I'm sorry."

"Thank you," Baynard said without sincerity. "Good day to you." He was turning away when a sight checked him. He pointed a finger beyond Stephen and shouted, "You!"

Stephen swung his head about. To his astonishment, Arnold Bromptone and Nigel FitzSimmons were approaching on foot down the slope from Ludford, followed by three armed men — the same men he'd seen at Bromptone's house.

"Don't you come any closer!" thundered Baynard.

"I'll go where I like," Bromptone said, drawing up. "And where I like is here, at the moment." He looked up at Stephen and said perfunctorily, "Attebrook. Good to see you well."

"I'm sure it is," Stephen said coolly. "And you, Sir Nigel."

FitzSimmons inclined his head all that politeness required.

"You're short a few men," Stephen said. "The one with that bad scar on his face — where is he?"

"He's been detained," FitzSimmons said through clenched teeth.

"A pity," Stephen said evenly.

"What do you want, Bromptone?" Baynard said.

"We heard about your misfortune," Bromptone said lightly. "Came to pay our condolences."

"Your condolences be damned."

"Well, you have them anyway, for what they're worth to you." Bromptone surveyed the ruins. "Quite a loss."

"I shall rebuild," Baynard grated.

"Commendable. It amazes me how merchants stand up to adversity."

"Life is risk."

"That it is. I came by to see if there isn't some accommodation to be reached in the matter of my son's contract and this claim for damages you have asserted."

Baynard grew angry and red. "You did this! Extortion! This is extortion!"

"Be careful what you say," Stephen said, shocked.

"This was arson, you idiot. And he means to profit by it."

"This was arson?" Stephen said.

"Of course, it was arson. Men were seen inside with torches last night before she went up!" Baynard snarled. He pointed his finger at Bromptone. "You! Your men!"

Bromptone looked grim. "You better be able to back that accusation up with action, Baynard."

"Action!" Baynard shouted, for he had lost all control of himself. "You'll have action!" He waved to his workmen. "These are the men who fired the mill! They took your jobs!"

The workers didn't need any further encouragement. They found staves and leaped the fence, scattering the boys, who, sensing a fight, dropped back so as not to be drawn into it but not so far that they didn't have a good view.

Bromptone and his friends drew swords.

In a moment, they'd be hacking at each other, blood would be flowing, and without a doubt, men would die here on this quiet lane. But Stephen was a king's officer, and could not allow that to happen.

Stephen drew his sword and spurred between the two factions. He shouted, "The king's peace! I declare the king's peace! As a crown officer, I order you to put those weapons down! There will be no brawling in the streets unless you want to answer to the sheriff!"

For a moment, Stephen thought the fight would erupt about him, but gradually, the weapons dipped toward the ground.

"That's better," Stephen snapped. "Now, disperse all of you, or I'll have the sheriff after you." The men glanced from him, to their adversaries, and to their leaders. Stephen snapped again, "Move! Rioting is a whipping offense, and I'll see it done, so help me God, if you don't disperse."

Baynard's eyes were on Bromptone when he spoke. "Saved by a cripple," he spat, and turned away. One by one, his men followed him through the fence, until only Stephen, Bromptone and his companions remained on the road.

Bromptone stood his sword on its point and folded his hands on the pommel. "It seems I am in your debt."

Stephen studied FitzSimmons, searching for some sign, anything that indicated he was behind the attempt to kill him. But FitzSimmons' eyes stayed on Baynard's back and he gave nothing away.

The Wayward Apprentice

"There is no debt," Stephen said. "This was duty. Now, all of you, be off, before there's more trouble."

Chapter 8

As Stephen directed the mare up the hill away from the mill, it occurred to him that he would pass close to Johanna's brew house. He had never been there, but had no trouble spotting it — long and low with a peaked thatched roof like all its neighbors but distinguished by the trestle tables in the yard where people liked to drink in good weather. The front door was open, revealing a narrow central corridor, which suggested that it had started its existence as a peasant cottage, the kind where the people lived on one side and the animals on the other, and he could see clear through the house and out the back to the yard and field beyond.

Stephen tethered the mare by the gate and crossed through the house to the back yard.

He saw a girl stirring a caldron which simmered over a fire, and three women raking barley malt in large pans in a shed. One of these women nudged another who straightened up, wiped her hands on her apron and came over.

"Is there something I can help you with?" the woman asked. She wasn't much older than Stephen and still pretty.

"I'm looking for Johanna," Stephen said.

"I'm Johanna," she said. She crossed her arms and regarded him warily. "What do you want? You obviously haven't come for the drink."

"No, but I'll try some just the same."

Johanna spoke to the girl at the caldron. "Pris, fetch his lordship a tankard." She turned back to Stephen. "What business does the coroner's new deputy have here?"

"You know."

"I've already told my story to Tom Pritcher and Alexander." They were two of the men on the coroner's jury. "I've nothing more to say."

"Patrick came, he drank, and he walked off," Stephen said.

"That's the size of it."

"You had no fight with him?"

"You accusing me now?"

"No, I'm asking."

"It was a busy night. We had no time to quarrel."

"And you heard nothing."

"Not even the whisper of the wind."

"What about the girls?"

"Only Pris was here that night. She's got nothing to add."

"Yet between this house and the ditch, someone stuck a knife in him. There's usually a reason for that, and it's most often a quarrel. I've never known a quarrel that didn't make noise."

She said, "He probably met someone on the road. There's a robber or two hereabout living in the woods. Could've been one of them."

"But that wasn't the way home."

"He probably got turned around in the dark. He'd had quite a few."

Pris came up with a wooden tankard. "Just tapped today," she said. She was a pretty thing, probably no more than fifteen with a small bud of a mouth that the boys must yearn to kiss. She looked troubled, lingering there as if she wanted to say something, but Johanna's glare drove her back to the caldron.

There was something about Pris, dark haired and brown eyed, that looked familiar, but Stephen could not put a finger on it what it was. He took a sip. The ale was fresh and sweet. "It's good," he said.

Johanna forced a thin smile. "Ain't poisoned a customer yet, governor."

He swirled the ale. Her coldness struck him as odd. He had no reason to doubt that she had once been Patrick's lover. Yet she did not seem moved. He said, "Aren't you sorry about Patrick? You were more than friends."

Johanna's eyes softened for a moment. She shrugged. "He was all right. Kinder than most." Then her eyes snapped back. "Look, governor, you finished? I got things to do. Don't have time to stand here."

"Don't let me interfere," Stephen said. It was obvious she wanted him to leave, but he just stood there, sipping the ale. When he didn't go, she turned back to raking barley mash.

Stephen strolled about the backyard. He wasn't sure why he did so, but he felt compelled to look the place over. Besides the equipment for brewing, the yard held a chicken coop and another enclosed shed. A peek in the shed's doorway brought him the separate stenches of pig and goat and the sight of separate pens for the animals.

He gazed across the field behind the shed, trying to spot the place where Patrick's body had been found. He imagined Patrick coming out of the brew house, crossing the yard, coming out near here and . . . what?

Whatever sign in the dirt of the yard of what transpired that night was long erased.

As he turned away from the field, he saw something that made him pause. Beyond the grass of the yard and a pair of the big spreading oaks that marked the boundary with the wheat field, he saw marks in the ground among the stubble. He left the yard and entered the field and knelt so as to put the marks between him and the rising sun.

They were man tracks, all right. It had been six days since Patrick had died. Most tracks that old would have been obliterated by now, but these had been set down in mud that had hardened after the rains, and were only now beginning to disappear. He knelt for a closer look, head near the ground. They were the footprints of men, two of them by the look of it, barely visible now, and partly covered by the marks of pigs. They had walked out into the margin of the field, together or apart, it was hard to tell, and then stopped to face each other. Then one set led off across the field. Stephen could not tell where the other man had gone.

He followed the footprints out into the field. Here and there, they disappeared. At the first disappearance he drew his sword and, going back to the last clear set, used the blade's length to measure the distance between right heel marks. It was a trick he had learned in Spain. Plotting distance on the ground with that measure, which told him where to expect to find another heel mark, he spotted one, an almost invisible half-moon impression nearly obliterated by a pig's print. Beyond it, he picked up the trail again. The marks zigged and zagged in a generally southwesterly direction toward the road to Richards Castle. A few more times, he lost the trail, but picked it up again.

Before he knew it, he had reached the road.

It was the same spot where Patrick had died.

There was no doubt in his mind that he had just followed Patrick's path to his death.

Stephen retraced his course across the field and entered the brew house yard. Johanna avoided his eye. He returned the tankard with a farthing to Pris.

He passed through the house again, and untied the mare. He allowed her a short drink in the trough, and then mounted her and started up the street toward the road.

It was clear Patrick hadn't been attacked in the field or at the road. Whoever had killed him had acted in the yard of the brew house. Johanna had to know more than she admitted. But he had no idea how to get her to talk. He'd think of something, somehow.

Chapter 9

The Canterbrigges' house lay on Berkeley Street, the main road that ran west to east straight through town, only a few doors down from Westgate. As with most merchant's houses, the shop lay on the ground floor facing the street. Through the open windows, Stephen could see that one side was occupied by looms, where half a dozen men and women clattered away with shuttles and cocks, weaving cloth. The clamor made him want to put a finger in his ears. The other side held racks displaying bolts of wool and linen in wildly different colors: blues, reds, deep rich maroons, forest greens, lush browns.

Stephen went in. A stooped old man wearing a fine green wool coat was behind the counter and asked his business.

"You're Walter Canterbrigge?" Stephen asked uncertainly. It had taken only one inquiry to learn of the man's name, for there could only be one Canterbrigge in Gloucester who was a draper.

"Oh, no, sir," the old man wheezed. "I'm Adam Oversee. The master is busy this morning. You can do all business with me that you can with him."

Stephen said, "I've ridden two days from Ludlow with a letter for his daughter," Stephen said. "Do you know where I can find her?"

"Two days from Ludlow! You must have flown on Pegasus." Adam's gnarled fingers groped the air. "You can give me the letter. I will deliver it."

"No," Stephen said. "I've been instructed to give it directly to her hands."

"Oh, such an important letter that must be," Adam said, each word a labored gasp. "I shall have to fetch the master. Yes, the master. He'll want to know about this." He tottered round the counter and headed toward the back hall, his mutterings gradually dwindling as he went deeper into the house: "Oh, yes, he'll want to know. A letter from Ludlow! From Ludlow! For Mistress Amicia . . . oh, my . . ."

Presently a heavy-set man appeared in the rear doorway followed at some distance by Oversee. This had to be Canterbrigge, with his distinguished gray hair and short beard, embroidered Lincoln green coat, its buttons silver rather than the more modest brass, and quite expensive black hose.

Canterbrigge introduced himself politely enough and held out his hand. "You've a letter for my daughter?"

Stephen said, "Master Wattepas in Ludlow asked me to deliver it personally."

Canterbrigge said coolly, "I'll see the letter."

"Master Wattepas was quite explicit. I was to deliver it to her alone." Stephen had been afraid of this, but there was no polite way he could refuse at least showing the letter to the girl's father. He drew it out, seal up, heart thumping with worry, for if Canterbrigge broke the seal and unfolded the leaf, he would find it blank. "He would be quite distressed if I violated his instructions."

"There is nothing Wattepas has to say to her that he could not say to me as well," Canterbrigge said. He took the letter and examined the seal closely. The perplexed and worried look in his eye told Stephen he recognized it. Stephen held his breath while Canterbrigge's finger strayed near the flap.

But Canterbrigge's hand dropped to his side. To Stephen's relief, he returned the letter with a sigh. Canterbrigge said, "Well, she's a married woman now. I suppose she's entitled to open her own letters." He smiled and relaxed. "It's hard for a father to let go, you know. But you wouldn't. You're too young."

"No, I wouldn't." Stephen breathed a little easier. "Can you tell me where she can be found?"

"If you came in from Ludlow on the west road, you passed the place. Her husband's shop is about a hundred yards this side of the Severn bridge. It's not large; he's just getting started in business. The sign is a spindle and ball of wool. Red wool."

Stephen surreptitiously took a deep breath. "Thank you."

Stephen sipped a mug of cider at a tavern across from Peter Bromptone's shop. A gnawed sweet bun lay on a napkin before him. Now that he had found young Bromptone, the prospect of dragging him back to three years of servitude weighed heavily on his conscience.

He did not have much time to dwell on his misgivings. Two beefy men wearing the sheriff's badge entered the inn and looked around. Stephen stood and beckoned to them. "Over here," he said.

"You have the writ, sir?" asked the taller of the two under-bailiffs, who introduced himself as Ralph.

Stephen waved a roll of parchment. "Yes."

"May I see it, please, sir?" the bailiff asked. Stephen was surprised he could read, but handed it over. The bailiff didn't tarry over the writing, however, pausing only to examine the seal. "Right, then. What about the money?"

Stephen put two pennies for each man on the table. Theoretically, bailiffs were not supposed to charge a fee for serving a writ for a crown officer, but they expected something nonetheless.

"Is there a chance we could get a spot of ale, your honor? It's such a hot day," the shorter bailiff asked, licking his lips and glancing toward the barrels at the other side of the room.

The request annoyed Stephen, but he waved over one of the serving girls, who fetched cups for the two men.

"Drink fast, boys," Stephen said. "I've got a long way to go."

Ralph drained his cup with great gulps. "Sure you don't want us to come with you?"

"I think I can manage." Having the two bailiffs as an escort back to Ludlow would cost him dearly and he didn't trust Baynard to cover all his expenses, especially if they were unexpectedly large.

"All right then," Ralph said. "You ready, Utti?"

Utti wiped off his dripping beard and grinned. "You sure you don't want him roughed up a bit?"

"I don't think that will be necessary," Stephen said.

"It helps when you soften 'em up. They give you less trouble."

"I don't think he's likely to cause any trouble."

"Never know about these boys," Utti said.

"He's a draper, not a mason."

"Yea, well, those young ones can be feisty, even the drapers. We've had our share of trouble with them."

"And he's married."

Utti looked disappointed. "They're as bad as the apprentices sometimes."

"I'm told this one's not a fighter, he's a talker." Stephen paid the bill and they crossed the street to Peter Bromptone's shop. Stephen paused at the door. The two bailiffs nearly bumped into him. He took a deep breath, and went in.

There was a single young man inside before a rack of woolen and linen cloth. He was a full six inches shorter than Stephen's rough hewn six feet and slender built. He had to be no more than twenty, brown haired with a spray of light freckles across his nose, but his boyish face made him look years younger. It was a handsome, friendly, open face, alight with eagerness at their appearance as if in anticipation of new business. Stephen was almost sorry to watch that eagerness melt away at the sight of the three hard men in the doorway.

"You're Peter Bromptone?" Stephen asked, just to be sure, although he was certain this was his man.

"I am," Peter said hesitantly. "How may I serve you?"

"My name is Stephen Attebrook. I am deputy coroner at Ludlow. I hereby attach you for abjuring your apprenticeship, for breach of contract, and for nonpayment of debt. You are under arrest and will answer at Ludlow. No sureties will be accepted." He motioned for the bailiffs to serve the writ.

Peter took the parchment with a hand that, surprisingly, was quite firm. He examined the writing. His eyes blazed. "That prick."

Utti, who had edged around to cut off a retreat through the rear door in case Bromptone thought to run, stepped forward menacingly. "Keep your tongue under control. You'll not talk to his honor that way!"

"This is my house, and I'll say what I like," Bromptone snapped.

Stephen couldn't help but smile. There was more iron in his spine than showed on his face.

Utti raised a fist, but Stephen stopped him. "Master Bromptone, you will have to come with me. If you have any things you wish to take with you that can be carried on the back of a horse, you'd best fetch them now."

Peter returned the writ to Stephen. "Very well," he said.

"Peter!" a woman's voice sounded from the rear doorway. "What's going on?"

They all turned to the new speaker. There was a moment of silence, a moment that to Stephen was tinged with awe. She was the most beautiful woman he had ever seen: lush brown hair piled above her head and covered with a matronly veil, a pale face under dark eyebrows with lively dark eyes that were narrowed with concern, hardly any nose at all, a delicate mouth and a pointed chin above a swan's neck. Beside her, Peter Bromptone was a pale shadow, and Stephen felt as plain as a lump of coal. No wonder Bromptone had thrown over his apprenticeship to marry her: she was beautiful enough to inspire murder.

Peter said bitterly, "This gentleman was come to arrest me, my dear. I'm to return to that man."

"Oh, dear god," Amicia said. "I can't believe it." Her voice was smooth and musical. Stephen felt the hair on his neck tingle at the sound of it.

"Baynard's malice has no limit," Peter said.

"I'll fetch father," Amicia said. "He'll put a stop to this."

Peter waved off this offer. He eyed Stephen and the bailiffs. "I doubt he can do anything to deter these hard men. They have a proper writ, and there's no way to avoid having to answer. It's all good law. I'm done, at least for now. Pack me a bag. The gentleman says we'll be riding directly."

Amicia nodded with sudden resolution and disappeared in the rear of the house. Stephen realized he hadn't taken his eyes off her since she had appeared. He must have gaped like a fool.

She returned within a quarter hour dressed in a traveling cloak and bearing two large satchels.

"What are you doing?" Peter asked in surprise.

"I'm going with you, of course."

"Amicia —" Peter said.

"No," she cut him off firmly. "I've made up my mind. I've written to father. He'll see to our affairs while we're gone and will send what aid he can." She turned to Stephen. "Sir, what are you waiting for? We're ready."

Chapter 10

Stephen and the Bromptones reached Ludlow on the evening of the 23rd as the bells of St. Laurence could be heard ringing curfew from across the river. Stephen had hoped they would arrive before the gates had been shut for the night, but they were bolted tight. He did not look forward to a moldy straw mattress at one of the lesser inns along the street, even if he was lucky enough to find one. So he continued up to the gate, where he rapped on it with the pommel of his sword.

"Who goes there?" the warden called, his voice muffled by the heavy oak panels.

"Stephen Attebrook, deputy coroner. I'm tired, and I don't want to be put to the expense of finding lodgings."

A small portal at head level swung inward. The warden's face appeared in the gap. "I'm not allowed to open the gates once curfew is rung," he said. "You know that."

Stephen slapped a half penny on the sill. "I won't tell anyone."

The warden regarded the half coin. "There's three of you." He squinted at Peter and Amicia. "I know him. He's Baynard's wayward apprentice. And she's the doxie he ran off with."

"Right," Stephen said. "And he's my prisoner. That means I have to pay toll for only two. Half a penny is more than enough."

The warden's tongue licked toothless gums. "All right," he said as Stephen reached for the half penny.

Bolts clanked and thudded, and the gate swung open just enough for one horse at a time to slip through. The warden stood momentarily in the gap, an old man so stooped that he looked as though he might topple over at any moment. He wagged a finger at Peter. "Ought not to be running away from your duties, young fellow." The warden cackled. "You'll be paying for it soon, I've no doubt."

"I'm sure you'd like to come and watch the fun, you old fart," Peter said sourly.

The warden glowered. "That's just the sort of back talk that got you in trouble in the first place. You need to learn to control your tongue."

"No reason to control it in front of you," Peter shot back.

"If I was younger, I'd thrash you good."

"But you're not, so you won't."

The warden grinned slyly. "Perhaps I'll have a word with my good friend Clement, then. He may speak to you for me."

At this threat, Peter's mouth tightened, and he said nothing.

Stephen grasped the rented horse's bridle and led the party up Broad Street and out of further danger from the warden, who hooted insults at Bromptone's back now that he had found a way to make the boy afraid.

"Horrible little man," Amicia said.

"They're all horrible," Peter said. "The whole town. They hate people like us. Now that the king's back in power, they think they can do anything to us they like."

"Oh, Peter," she said and clasped him more tightly around the waist. "I thought, I really thought we might be free."

He patted her hands affectionately. "We'll be free again soon. Don't you worry about that."

"But how soon?"

"I don't know. But we'll manage."

"I know your father won't help, but mine will. He'll come."

"Baynard's price will be too high for him too, I'm afraid. We'll endure, that's what we'll do."

"I hope so."

Baynard's house lay on College Lane a hundred yards or so north of St. Laurence's church, hard against the town wall. It was an unusual house for Ludlow in that the ground floor was made of gray stone, with black and white timber-and-plaster floors looming above another four stories to a peaked blue slate roof. Stephen dismounted at the front door and unlocked the chain holding Peter to the saddle, but did not unfetter his wrists.

Peter held up his hands, however, and said, "Come on, unfasten me. I'll not run anywhere."

One might think that, because he'd have to leave his wife behind if he ran, he would stay and take his medicine. But Stephen had known men who'd abandon their women in lesser circumstances. He still hesitated.

"Please," Peter said. "Don't take me in there ironed like a common criminal."

Stephen understood the humiliation irons would cause. He fumbled for the key and unfastened Peter's arms.

"Thank you," Peter said. He rubbed his wrists where the irons had chaffed them.

Stephen lifted the big round iron door knocker and let it fall several times. Presently the door cracked open. Stephen had a glimpse of a slightly built man whose remaining gray hair had long strands combed over his bald dome. He was better dressed than an ordinary servant. "Who may I ask is calling?" the man inquired.

"Stephen Attebrook."

The servant looked beyond Stephen to his companions. "Ah, young Bromptone. Good to see you again."

"I can't say I have the same pleasure, Muryet," Peter said sourly.

Muryet ignored the venom. "Please come in."

They followed Muryet into the house. The front part of the ground floor of the houses of most merchants held a shop, but this house was different. There was no shop here; Stephen understood that Baynard was so well to do that he held three houses in the town. One of them was his principal place of business, one he rented, and this one, his grandest, he lived in. The front door here opened into a small hallway flanked by a sitting room with a fireplace on the right. On the left was what appeared to be a coat room. Beyond the entryway, the hall proper opened up. It was a high-ceilinged room that rose in the center to the rafters, which were painted blue, with yellow stars. A massive stone fireplace dominated the far end and a slightly smaller one overlooked the right.

The family and servants were at supper, the tables arranged in the hall in the shape of a U. Baynard presided in the center before the main fireplace so he enjoyed its full effect. He laid his hands on each side of his trencher and glared at Peter with satisfaction.

"Peter, how good to see you," Baynard said with mock warmth.

"I cannot say the same," Peter said.

"Still not tamed, I see. Can't you learn something from the fact you are here? Or are you too thick headed to take a lesson?"

"What would that lesson be?"

"That I am the master and I will be obeyed, and you will show proper obedience and respect while in my service."

"And if not?"

"Then you will suffer for it. There is no avoiding either the lesson or the service."

"I could run again."

"You could. But next time I will sue for your surety. You may recall, it's twenty pounds. Your father hasn't twenty pounds to his name. He'd have to pledge the manor to pay the judgment. I'm sure your family won't appreciate the fact you've made them homeless."

"I'll buy the contract.

"I won't sell."

"You just want to humiliate us, those who stand for justice and reason, and against tyranny!"

Baynard slammed his hand on the table. "I'll not have treason spoken in my house, boy!" He twitched a finger in the air. "Fetch the switch. Words aren't enough to penetrate his skull. He needs a lesson he will remember."

A servant left the table and raced to the rear of the house. He returned with a long wooden rod, which he handed to Clement, who rose and swished the air viciously.

Peter went pale. Amicia grasped his arm. He squeezed her hand and stepped away from her.

"On your knees," Baynard said. "Repent your words and speak your loyalty to the king."

Peter didn't move.

Clement came round the table and kicked Peter behind the knee. The blow collapsed his legs and he fell to hands and knees.

"Can't you do anything to stop this?" Amicia implored Stephen.

Hardfaced, Stephen crossed his arms. He said, "It's Baynard's legal right to discipline his apprentices. I have no warrant to interfere."

Amicia's hands went to her face and she turned away as Clement raised the rod two-handed over his head.

"Give him ten," Baynard said with savage satisfaction.

Stephen winced, remembering what it was like to receive ten lashes with such a rod.

Clement nodded. He brought the rod down hard on Peter's back. Peter cried out. Clement struck him again. Peter shrieked and curled into a ball.

Clement spat with disgust. "Take your medicine like a man, boy."

Eight more times the rod rose and fell. Peter whimpered at each blow. Clement counted each one, and when he reached ten, he raised his hand for another.

"Enough," Baynard said.

Clement wiped sweat from his forehead. He seemed disappointed.

Baynard said, "Are you ready to accept Henry as your rightful king?"

Peter mumbled, "We've always accepted our lord as the rightful king. He's just ill served and ill advised."

"Give him another ten," Baynard said.

"You've a right to discipline him, not kill him," Stephen said suddenly.

Baynard stared at Stephen as if surprised he was still here. "What did you say?"

"I said, you've a right to beat him, not kill him."

"I've a right to punish treason."

"No, that right belongs to the sheriff and our lord's justices. If you believe he is a traitor, then report him and let the law deal with him. But I think he's had enough. And he's acknowledged Henry as the rightful king. That isn't treason."

Baynard's fingers played nervously with his table knife, a thunderous expression on his face. Evidently few dared to challenge Baynard. He appeared about to burst, but he managed to contain himself. With some effort, he turned back to his supper. He cut a slice of pork and chewed on it. Then he said, "Are you ready to behave now?"

Peter nodded.

"Clement, show Peter his room," Baynard said. "Don't let any harm come to him on the way. Our coroner here will be watchful."

"Right, sir." Clement took Peter by the arm and hauled him to his feet. "Try not to puke on the floor," he said to Peter. "We've just cleaned it."

Peter looked at him with pain-filled eyes.

Clement led him away.

Amicia tried to follow, but Stephen caught her by the arm and held her back. She shook him off with a glare.

In the quiet that followed Peter's departure, the accountant Elyas emerged from the shadows behind him bearing a small leather purse. Elyas held it out to Stephen, who hesitated, feeling soiled and conscious of Amicia's eyes. Then he put out his hand, and Elyas dropped the purse into his palm.

Baynard waved toward one of the tables. "You are welcome to stay for supper as well. But not the wench."

"Your hospitality is poison," Amicia said proudly. "I wouldn't want it."

Baynard said, "Go back to Gloucester, bitch."

Face aflame with humiliation, Amicia wheeled about and marched toward the front door.

Stephen turned to follow her.

"You'll not be staying?" Baynard asked Stephen without a trace of disappointment.

"I don't think so. I'm tired and anxious to get home."

"Thank you for your help," Baynard said with a nod and false politeness

Amicia stood crying in the middle of the street. Stephen nearly put his arm around her, but the gesture would be unwelcome, so he just stood by feeling useless.

"Where will you go?" Stephen asked.

Amicia wiped her cheeks with her fingers. Her white face shone in the brilliant glow of a half moon. "I shall go see Mistress Wattepas. I shall convince her to take me in." She faced him and added, "That is what I will do."

Without waiting for his reply, she marched off toward High Street.

It was clear that she did not want his help, and he should have gone home. She didn't need an escort in Ludlow, even after dark, for unlike larger towns there was not much crime once the curfew took hold.

But he followed slowly at a distance, guessing at the reception Amicia likely would receive at the Wattepas house.

He lingered at the corner for a long time, watching her dark figure glide in and out of moon shadows and then slip through the silvery band of light in the center of the deserted street. She reached the Wattepas house and merged with its dark shape. He heard the door knocker thud distantly. A flash of candlelight indicated the opening and closing of the door.

The mare nudged his shoulder and snickered to tell him she was hungry and wanted to be fed. "Just a moment longer, sweetheart," he murmured to her.

But the moment stretched into two, then three, and then at least a quarter hour — so long that he was able to notice how the moon shadows had moved on the ground.

At last, the Wattepases' front door opened and a slender figure emerged into the street.

She started when she saw him, as if she did not know who it was, but she relaxed, and said bitterly, "They will not have me back."

Stephen nodded. "Runaway servants, like runaway apprentices, are rarely trusted again."

"I didn't mean to betray them!"

Stephen turned the horses toward Mill Street. "Come on. There's a bed waiting for you at the Broken Shield."

"I can't pay. We had so little and I left it all with my father to keep the shop going." She shuddered. "I'll have to sleep on the street. People do it. I've seen them."

"No, you won't."

Stephen turned toward home. At first, she didn't follow. Then she hurried to catch up.

They walked in silence the rest of the way to the inn.

Stephen pushed open the door to the Broken Shield to find Edith, Gilbert, and a couple of the girls tidying up the hall, the unavoidable chore that put a cap on every working day. Edith was mopping behind the bar, Jennifer and another girl were wiping tables with wet rags, and Gilbert was harrying dust balls on the floor with a broom. The only remaining patrons, a half dozen men and a couple of girls, slouched in a corner over a backgammon game.

Edith was a demon on saving candles after dark as much as they could, so the only light came from a trio of low-burned candles placed at intervals about the hall. It was so dark in places that it was amazing Edith could find a lick of dirt, but somehow she always managed and never failed to point it out to Gilbert or the girl who'd missed it. In the morning the hall would appear spotless, its dark brown wood shiny.

Gilbert put up his broom with enthusiasm and bustled to greet them. "My boy, you're home, and safe! You must be tired and hungry. Jennie, fetch some of the bean soup. I'm sure there's some left —"

"Probably burned to the bottom of the pot by now if it hasn't been fed to the pigs," Jennie muttered as she departed for the kitchen.

"— and bread — the white, not the black — you hear!" Gilbert went on. "Hurry now." He conducted Stephen and Amicia over to a table and took a seat across from them. "Now, tell me your news. And you are?" he asked Amicia.

"Gilbert," Stephen said, "may I present Mistress Amicia Bromptone." He added further introductions for Edith, Sam the maid, and the absent Jennifer.

Gilbert's forehead wrinkled with the effort of remembering. "Bromptone? Bromptone did you say?" His finger stood upright. "Not a relation to —"

"I believe you are thinking of my husband," Amicia said with dignity that seemed odd in one so young. She couldn't be more than seventeen.

"Peter Bromptone!" Gilbert finished. "I didn't know he was married. How could he be married? He's an apprentice."

"He took it upon himself to change his situation," Stephen said.

"Ah," Gilbert said. "That explains why he left Baynard."

"In part, perhaps," Stephen said. He thought that Amicia might add something, but she just clasped her hands on the table top and looked into a corner. So he said, "It seems there's bad blood between Baynard and the Bromptones." Quickly he told the story of the altercation at the mill the day he left Ludlow.

"Yes," Gilbert said slowly. "I heard about that. You're lucky you weren't killed. They could easily have come to blows."

Jennie returned with a tray bearing two steaming bowls and sliced bread, which she placed in front of them. The stew did not smell or taste the least bit burnt, despite her misgivings. Stephen and Amicia dug in.

After a few spoonfuls, Stephen said, "Amicia needs a situation herself. The Wattepases won't take her back."

"Oh, dear," Gilbert said. "I will have to think about that. Who would do? Indeed, who would do?"

Edith leaned on her mop. "We could use another girl," she said.

"I don't know." Amicia sounded doubtful.

Stephen wondered about that too. It was one thing for girls from good merchant families to go into service — it was the main way they could earn dowries. It was another to become a tavern girl.

Edith of course understood but took no offense. "If not that, I could use another laundress."

"Well," Amicia said reluctantly, "perhaps. If only for a while. Until I find something more suitable."

"I'll ask Sir Geoff when he gets back," Stephen said. "He'll know someone. No reason why you have to stick with the town."

Amicia said, "I would be forever grateful."

Stephen said, "She'll need a place to stay in the meantime."

"Naturally," Edith said. "There's a spare bed in Sarah's room. You can sleep there."

"Thank you so much."

Edith smiled. "Perhaps you'll think differently when you get those pretty hands chapped at the washboard."

In the corner, the backgammon game erupted into a fistfight. The table tipped over, the board went flying, and the game pieces scattered along the money. Spectators scrambled on the floor for the coins, while the two fighters stood toe to toe slugging it out.

Gilbert's jolly demeanor evaporated in an instant. Edith tossed him a stout oak stave as long as a man's arm, which

Gilbert caught with practiced ease. He rushed to the fighters with Stephen right behind to back him up.

But Stephen wasn't needed. Gilbert grabbed the nearest fighter on the shoulder and kicked him behind the knee, which brought the man to the ground. Then Gilbert struck the other man a hard two-handed blow on the shoulder. The victim of his blow shrank back, holding his shoulder and whining.

"Be glad that wasn't your head," Gilbert said. "Now get out of here — all of you."

"But our money," one of them protested.

"You know there's no fighting in the Shield. You can come back for it tomorrow when you've had a chance to cool off." He wagged the staff at the people on their knees. "And you — drop every pence. Now! I'm watching you like a hawk. And I'll break any man's — or woman's — head who doesn't comply."

Gilbert's threats were not empty, as they all knew from previous experience, so coins that had found their way into fists and purses clattered on the floorboards. Gilbert said, "That's better. The door's that way. Stephen will show you the way, in case you've forgotten."

Stephen grinned. He bowed them toward the door in his best imitation of a butler. "Gentlemen, ladies, may I escort you . . ."

The guests had no option but to comply and they trooped out sullenly. "I'll be counting it tomorrow morning!" one of them said in a parting shot on the threshold. "I want a full accounting! It best be all there!"

"Don't you be suggesting I'm a thief, Adam Fitzowen," Gilbert shouted back.

Stephen cut off any further rejoinders by shoving the last of the group through the door. He followed them out and stood at the doorstep, arms crossed, to make sure they dispersed. As they disappeared into the shadows, muttering and grumbling, he called through the closed door, "You can bar up. I've got the horses to tend to. I'll be in shortly."

He went through the gate to the yard, where he paused to drop the bar on the gate. The two mares were waiting patiently at a water trough by the side door, which was disconcerting because he'd left them tied at a post by the gate. He wondered how they had come loose. He had been tying horses to posts since he was a child and had never had this happen. He pulled the double doors open, standing back to allow them to swing free, and paused at the black cavernous entrance. It was so dark he couldn't see a thing. He wished now he had thought to bring a candle.

"Harry," he called, "you asleep?"

"Nay," Harry's voice came from somewhere on the left. "How can a man sleep with all the racket you're making?"

"Which stalls are free?"

"There's two on the right at the wall not taken."

"Thanks."

"Don't mention it."

He groped his way to the right, found the stalls, and put one mare in the first and the other in the second. Light from the moon splashed in the open doorway and gradually, as his eyes grew accustomed to the dark, vague shapes began to emerge. There was a thumping from the left and Harry clumped through into the rectangle of light. "Need some help there?" he asked.

"Anything for a penny, eh, Harry?"

"Man's got to eat. I was good with horses, once. Would have made a good groom, if the lord had given me a chance."

"Are there any oats left?"

"Ought to be. Gilbert had half a dozen sacks in day before yesterday."

Stephen leaned his sword against the wall and found the oats in their bin. He scooped twice into a bucket, which he put on the hay in the older mare's stall. She went for it immediately, and he had to warn her off, "Slow down, girl. I've got to get that tack off first."

Stephen removed the bridle and let her go to the bucket while he unhitched the saddle girth.

He was lifting the saddle to a saw horse beside the stall gate when Harry slapped him on the thigh and hissed, "Quiet!"

"What's going on?"

"There's someone in the yard," Harry whispered urgently.

"What's odd about that?"

"They don't belong. Listen!"

Stephen couldn't hear anything untoward at first but the sighing of the wind. Then he heard a faint, snick, snick, snick. Coming this way. Not the sort of careless noise an ordinary person might make when crossing the yard, but the furtive, cautious sound of someone trying to move quietly and in a bit too much of a hurry.

A voice murmured beyond the door.

Then two men slipped into the rectangle of silver light at the doorway.

"'Scuse me," one of the men said at the sight of them, "but are there any rooms at the inn for the night? We knocked on the door but nobody answered." The two men did not wait for a reply. They came toward Stephen with elaborate casualness. They obviously wanted to put Stephen off his guard, but everything about them screamed threat.

Harry grabbed Stephen's calf in alarm.

Stephen edged away from Harry, trying to keep the light behind the two men. They weren't armed, except for knives. But that was bad enough, if they were what he thought. Two against one in a knife fight was a losing proposition for the one.

He looked desperately for his sword, but the two men were even with the place where he'd left it. There was no chance now that he could get to it if they meant to attack. And they were so close that he dared not look around for another weapon because they'd be on him if he turned to search for one.

He was trying to make up his mind what to do when they attacked.

The one on his right grasped his arm and the man on the left drew his knife. It seemed like a move they had practiced before: one to hold the victim immobile and the other to do the butchering. Quick and certain death. But Stephen knew tricks from hundreds of hours spent wrestling in castle baileys and village churchyards, and they came easily to his mind. He moved to the right almost before the first man had a complete grasp on his sleeve and coat. He levered the near elbow upward, grasped the hair at the top of the head, and pitched his nearest attacker to the ground in the path of the knifer. The knifer stumbled and fell to his knees with a curse. Stephen aimed a kick with his bad foot at the knifer's head but struck a rock-like shoulder instead. The impact was intense and Stephen nearly cried out. But there wasn't time for that kind of weakness. The knifer stabbed at Stephen's legs but he only snagged a big hole in a stocking.

For a moment, Stephen saw what he had hoped to create — a way clear around the attackers to the open door. Just a few, brief steps. That's all he'd need to be away and safe.

But then Harry propelled himself forward with surprising speed and was upon the first man and wrestling on the ground.

If Stephen ran now, they'd kill Harry just to get away.

He couldn't leave.

Stephen swept the saddle off the saw horse and threw it at the knifer.

The saddle struck the knifer full in the chest and it carried him backward to the ground.

Stephen drew his own dagger as the knifer threw off the saddle. He kicked at Stephen's legs to keep him away, and only when Stephen had danced back did he rise.

They measured each other for a few moments. Then the knife-man attacked with a quick lunge at the belly. It was a fake because as Stephen reacted, he shifted the blow to the head. Stephen barely twisted aside in time to avoid the blade, the man's arm so close that the hair on his forearm brushed Stephen's cheek. Without conscience thought, Stephen's own blade lanced out for the man's ribs, but a hand caught Stephen's forearm in an iron grip. For a moment, it seemed that Stephen was finished, for the other's blade drew back for the killing stroke. But Stephen twisted his hand to slice at the man's arm as he delivered the killing blow, Stephen set it aside with his free hand, and there followed such a rapid and improbable exchange of blow, parry, and counter-blow, of turn and avoidance, of push and step, that no spectator would have believed it possible, for knife fights never as a rule last more than seconds before one of the antagonists is bleeding on the ground.

The flow of battle put the knife-man between Stephen and the door again. At a brief pause, the knife-man realized this, and he turned and ran. Stephen heard his footfalls across the yard to the front gate, then a shuddering of wood as he vaulted over to the street and was gone.

Stephen turned back to help Harry. He and the other assailant were locked in a death struggle side by side on the ground. The attacker had pulled his knife, but Harry had caught his arm with one hand. With the other hand Harry clasped the man by the throat. Harry's eyes were wild, his nostrils flared, his teeth bared in a soundless snarl. The other man's face made Stephen want to turn away. The eyes bulged, the mouth distended as if in a scream cut off by the massive strength in Harry's hands.

Stephen knelt beside them. "Harry," he said, "you can let go now."

Harry glared insanely at him, panting through clenched teeth.

"He's finished, Harry," Stephen said. He took the dagger from the dead man's hand and laid it on the ground. Gently he worked at Harry's fingers.

Slowly Harry came back to earth. The panting subsided. The mad gleam in his eyes began to fade. The rigidity in his great arms slacked. He allowed Stephen to pry his hand lose from the man's throat and sagged onto his back.

"I killed him?" Harry said.

"Yes."

"I never killed a man before."

"There's always a first time for everything."

"It's homicide. I'll have to answer. A man like me — I'll never get a pardon."

The law was precise and implacable on this point. Every homicide required the killer to stand trial. Pleas of self defense were not enough to avoid the gallows. Only a king's pardon could buy that, and pardons cost much in money and influence.

"Don't worry about it," Stephen said.

He went to the door and took a deep breath of the chill night air. The town and the inn were silent under blazing stars and a half moon. A dog barked in the distance. A woman laughed in the neighboring house. Nobody, it seemed, had any inkling that violent death had occurred in this ordinary place.

Stephen went back into the stables. Harry's hands were cupped over his face.

"How can I run without legs?" Harry said.

"You'll not need to run anywhere," Stephen said. "You're going to bed, where you should have stayed in the first place." He offered his hand to help Harry sit up, but Harry ignored it and levered himself upright. Stephen turned toward the other side of the stables, where Harry lived but stopped in the doorway.

"If anybody asks," Stephen said as Harry lumbered by, "I killed him."

Chapter 11

Gilbert examined the dead man in the light of his candle. With this illumination, it was possible now to see that the corpse had an unpleasant, rat-like face marked from small pox. He wore a much-patched brown coat and stockings that had once been green.

"Good Lord," Gilbert sighed. "You've a penchant for trouble, my boy."

"Any idea who he is?" Stephen asked.

"No, I'm afraid not."

Harry shuffled into the light for a closer look. "I know him," he croaked.

"Oh?" Gilbert asked in an interested tone.

"Name's Simon Butcher, though he's not a butcher. His dad was. He works — or worked — at the mill that burned last week."

"Baynard's mill," Stephen said, surprised.

"Yes," Harry said. "He's a loud mouth, a drunk, and a braggart. Kicked me once for no reason."

"Not someone who would be missed," Gilbert said in a musing tone. "A wife? Children?"

"There's a wife and three," Harry said, "but he don't live with 'em. She threw him out because of drink. He had a doxy in Ludford, but I heard even she's gone too now."

"Ah," Gilbert said contemplatively.

"With the mill burned, he probably needs money," Stephen said.

"He's the kind who always needs money," Harry said. "Makes an extra penny or two collecting debts and beating people up. He's especially fond of opponents of the king."

Gilbert said, "Too many of that kind in this town and not the sort Fitzsimmons or Bromptone would turn to."

"He'd kill his mother for a penny," Harry added.

"Well, then, perhaps I'm wrong," Gilbert said. "It's a pity he's not here to tell us who put him up to this. You didn't have to kill him, did you?"

There was a pause. Then Stephen said, "I lost my head."

"A pity," Gilbert said again. "Well, there's the question of what do we do now."

"What else is there to do?" Stephen said. He wondered if his cousin could be prevailed on to pay for the pardon once he was convicted of homicide. "We'll have to inform the sheriff and convene a jury."

Gilbert stood up and blew out the candle. "You know," he said, "that old latrine needs burning out again. Funny how they get so filthy so quickly." He turned to Stephen. "There's a pile of rubble by the back fence. Go fetch a couple of stones. Big ones. We don't want our friend here floating to the surface if we can help it. And wipe that look off your face. You don't want to be found out, do you?"

Chapter 12

The knock on the door seemed to come almost as soon as he put his head on the pillow. Stephen's eyes flew open. The first thing he thought was, someone's found the corpse in the latrine.

The knock sounded again, more insistent.

Stephen thought about jumping from the window, but he was naked and the fall was too far in any case. He wrapped a blanket around himself and drew the dagger from under the pillow.

Then he cracked the door, prepared to fight if anyone barged in.

Amicia regarded him with surprise and alarm: not because of the dagger, because he held it out of sight, but because of the blanket and his obvious nakedness.

She studied a corner. "I've been asked to summon you for mass," she said.

No one having found a dead man in a latrine would say something as commonplace as that. "Mass," he croaked.

"Yes, mass," Amicia said, continuing to study a point outside his room.

"You're going now?"

"That is the mistress' desire."

"What time is it?" Stephen asked.

"Almost time for Terce."

"Ah." It was hard not being physically affected by her presence, which was accompanied by the aroma of some clean flowery scent he could not place.

The door had swung open slightly while he stood there, wits dulled, and he heard Amicia gasp. He saw she was looking at the bare stump of his left foot.

He drew the foot out of sight, embarrassed.

"I'm sorry," she said.

"About what?"

"Your ..."

"Foot."

"Yes."

"Just some bad luck. A Moor cut it off. With an axe."

Amicia winced. "It's God's will."

Stephen snorted.

Amicia was shocked. "That's blasphemy."

Stephen put a finger to his lips. "Don't tell anyone."

She started to turn away. "You won't be attending mass, then, I see."

He said, "I'll come."

"It will do you good," she said firmly.

"Edith says that too," Stephen said. He closed the door to a mere crack. "I'll be right down. Have to get dressed first."

"That would be wise."

Amicia was waiting by the door with the rest of the Wistwodes, so Stephen gave up on the thought of breakfast and followed them out to the street.

At Broad Street they turned uphill toward the parish church. Terce was the most popular time for Sunday mass and there were streams of people headed the same way. By the time they reached the churchyard, the streams had congealed into a crowd.

Amicia stopped abruptly just short of the church entrance. Stephen had gone two paces beyond her before he realized she was not at his side. He turned to look for her and found her glaring at Anselin Baynard, who stalked by with his wife, daughters, servants, and apprentices forming a rather formidable procession in his wake.

Amicia smiled, for there was Peter at the tail end of the parade, with a bruise on his left cheek. Amicia gasped and hurried to him. She put delicate fingers to his face and traced the edges of the bruise.

"My dear," she said anxiously, "what more have they done to you?"

"Nothing," Peter said evasively. His hands twitched as if he wanted to embrace her. But such a public display was unseemly, so he contented himself with devouring her with his eyes. "I'm fine. Where are you staying?"

"At the Broken Shield," she said, gesturing at Stephen. "Your captor graciously found a place for me."

Peter looked guardedly at Stephen and was about to say something when a voice cracked, "Bromptone! Come here!"

Peter's head snapped around. "Coming!" He said swiftly to Amicia, "I'll see you again tonight. I'll get away after dark."

"Oh, I shall count the hours!"

Peter hurried through the church doors after Baynard.

Amicia turned to Stephen. "Well, sir, shall we go in, or have you put down roots?"

There was nothing you could say to a woman in a mood like this, so Stephen just followed her into church.

Despite all the troubles and distractions, thoughts of Patrick the carter were never far from Stephen's mind. He had mulled the man's seemingly pointless death on the ride to Gloucester and on the return, had reviewed all the evidence in his mind, and had only the conclusion to nourish him that Johanna the brewer must know more than she was willing to tell. How to make her part with what she might know was a challenge for which he had no solution. Some men were clever at such things, but Stephen was not and he knew it.

He thought about these things again when he went out to the stables after dinner. He passed Harry, who was sunning himself by the woodpile, whittling on a stick.

"Don't go there," Harry said quietly without looking up from his whittling. At the corner, one had the choice of proceeding left to the latrine, or right to the stables.

Stephen paused. He saw Harry had fashioned a rather clever little figure of a man at the end of the stick. The figure was holding his mouth with both hands and had a look on his face as if he had seen something ghastly.

When Stephen didn't promptly answer, Harry said, "I've dug a little hole round behind the stable. I don't mind sharing."

"It would look odd, don't you think?"

"Don't seem right. It's bad enough we had to put him in the pit."

"Are you having an attack of conscience, Harry?"

"I got no conscience."

"Good, because neither have I." Stephen stepped around Harry and continued to the stable door, where he paused again. "Harry," he called over the woodpile.

"What? Have you no eyes, man? Can't you see I'm busy?"

"What do you know about Johanna, that brew mistress in Ludford?"

"Not too much. I don't get over to Ludford often, you know, owing to my situation."

"Well, you must meet Ludford folks coming in Broad Gate."

"Oh, sure, and they love to stop and gossip with me."

"Well, keep an ear open about her just the same, will you?"

"Oh, yeah, I sure will." Harry's voice took on a high sing-song: "Oh, say, Mark, my boy, you remember that carter fellow what got killed at Johanna's place over to Ludford way, don't you? Right, heard he was sweet on her. Could she have taken another lover, then, you think — that's it, a jealous lad, who didn't take kindly to Patrick's attentions. Don't say. Think he slipped a knife in the boy's ribs, then? Ah, I bet she's covering up for him then, eh?"

"Harry, you'll have my place before long," Stephen said.

"And no doubt do a better job than you."

Stephen turned the mare into Broad Street. It was a warm Sunday afternoon, and Broad, like High Street a location for fashionable houses, had more than its share of strollers about seeing and being seen and getting in the way of a rider who wanted to go somewhere without interruption. One large crowd had gathered before the gate where the ground was level to watch a dozen boys playing football. Stephen had to maneuver the mare around the edges of the crowd to reach the gate, which stood open and unguarded.

Beyond the gate the houses were smaller and more modest. Working people lived here, weavers and dyers, mostly. At St. John's Hospital a friar sweeping the stoop glowered at him. Stephen waved at the friar, who made no reply and bent over his broom. Even though it was Sunday, it seemed there was no rest for the mendicant.

The horse mounted the bridge at a slow walk, horseshoes clinking on the cobbles of the pavement. The rhythmic pace was soothing. Stephen let her set her own pace and admired the view from the top of the bridge. At this spot above the river, he felt as though he was a bird flying through the air. Only the heights at Whitcliffe revealed more beauty about Ludlow than this.

Stephen's eyes fell on the weirs off to the left. They consisted of banks of earth shaped like an arms of the letter V with the point aimed at him, stretching across the river, directing the river flow to the mills on either side of the stream.

A figure stepped out of the foliage on the town side and trotted across the weir. Stephen recognized the boy as Patrick's son, Edgar. As Edgar reached the Ludford side, a girl came out of a thicket to meet him. Stephen realized with a bit of a start that it was that tavern girl, Pris. The couple clasped hands and ran into a stand of trees by the burned mill.

Stephen passed the peak of the bridge and began the descent toward Ludford. Within moments he would be mounting the slope and then within a few moments more he'd be at the doorstep of Johanna's brew house, and he had no idea what he was going to say to her or how he was going to make her open up.

He heard a clattering of hooves on the bridge pavement. Gilbert's head and that of his mule bounced into view. Gilbert saw him and waved. "Stephen, stop!"

Stephen reined in and waited for him at the foot of the bridge. Gilbert trotted up, holding tightly to the saddle, looking anxious.

"What is it, Gilbert?" Stephen asked.

"There's been another death," Gilbert said. "The hundred bailiff wants you to come immediately. There is a crowd and he's afraid of things being disturbed."

The dead man's name was Bernard Gilley, and there could be no doubt that he had broken his neck. He lay sprawled beside a tumbledown cottage on Broad Linney, a street that ran north from town almost as far as the River Corve, surrounded by a crowd of as many as sixty men, women, and children. Everyone there had a story to tell about Bernard and how and why he died, and they were so eager to talk that they couldn't be encouraged to wait for the assembly of the coroner's jury. It was enough to try even Gilbert's prodigious memory.

It seemed that Bernard had not been right in the head for many years. He lost his job as a saddle maker and lived with his mother. He began to neglect himself so that he was as filthy as the meanest beggar. He had intense conversations with invisible people. At first, these conversations were whispered and furtive, but eventually he was often seen on the street waving his hands and shouting, as if he was followed by ghosts only he could see. Once he attacked a girl in her yard and beat her rather badly before her brothers drove him off. Only the fact that he was cracked saved him from prosecution and a fine, and even so, his mother had given the girl's family a share of milk from the family cow for three months to make amends.

Day before yesterday, Bernard attacked the family cow with a knife and wounded it — a serious matter because the cow was the mother's only source of income. His mother came to the cow's rescue and drove Bernard away with a stick. He retreated to the roof of the cottage, where he was heard shouting things in which only a word or two could be made out now and then.

Bernard had been tolerated as generally harmless, even after the incident with the girl, and largely ignored whenever possible, but his latest escapade attracted considerable attention. Because Friday and Saturday were workdays, only young children had gathered to watch at first. The children were ready with piles of rocks, which they threw at him.

Bernard did not come down after dark, even when the children had all gone home. Bernard's mother had got over the attack on the cow when it appeared it would live, and she implored him to come to supper and bed, but Bernard was too busy with his conversations.

On Sunday, being a day off, a large crowd gathered after terce mass to witness the spectacle. It was alleged that a number of people threw rocks at Bernard. But no names were mentioned and no one owned up to being a guilty party. Everyone present was very firm on the point that the rock throwing had nothing to do with Bernard's end.

The unanimous opinion was that Bernard met his fate by accident. He began pacing along the peak of the roof from one end of the house to the other. To the encouragement of the crowd, Bernard sang and capered more intensely. An improvident step, a stumble, and then a tumble brought Bernard to the ground, where he landed on his head, to shocked silence. Everyone had wanted a little fun, but not this.

Making sense of it all took several hours. Then Stephen had Bernard carried into his house and laid him on the dinner table, where they stripped the corpse and gave it a thorough examination. Although there didn't seem to be any doubt that the fall had killed Bernard, Stephen wasn't about to cut corners after what had happened in the Patrick Carter case.

It was twilight when Stephen and Gilbert rode slowly back up Broad Linney to town.

"I wonder what's for supper," Stephen said, glad to be relieved of thoughts of death.

"Whatever it is, I'm in a hurry to get it," Gilbert said. "Investigating works up a hunger."

Stephen glanced to the west, where the sun had already set. "We'd better hurry. They'll be closing the gates soon. I haven't enough money left to get us both in."

Stephen asked for a canter and his mare surged forward.

"By all means," Gilbert replied to Stephen's back, "we must bustle." He thumped the mule's sides but with perhaps too much vigor.

Knowing it was pointed in the direction of home and eager for its own supper, the mule burst into a furious gallop. It quickly swept by Stephen, with Gilbert clutching the pommel. He bounced and swayed so much that Stephen feared he'd take to the air and land on his head. It would be bad enough having to explain such a mishap to the coroner's jury — but to Edith? Stephen shuddered.

He dashed in pursuit when it was obvious that the mule had no intention of slowing down. Linney Gate, which pierced the town wall at the foot of Broad Linney street, was still open, but it was so narrow and low that a prudent mule ordinarily could be expected to check its speed to get through. Not this mule. Gilbert had so encouraged his mount that the prospect of the gate had no effect, and it careered through into College Lane with Gilbert bent low to avoid losing his head on the lintel.

"Oh, damn," Stephen muttered, as he pushed the mare to maintain her gallop.

He shot through the gate, nearly colliding with a figure emerging from Baynard's house who threw himself out of the way.

Stephen, thinking he had almost trampled Peter Bromptone on his way to Amicia, shouted an apology as he raced by, but he couldn't spare an instant for more civilities if he was to catch the mule before Gilbert fell off.

He finally apprehended it at the corner of High Street, and managed to bring it to a halt.

"Well," Gilbert said, "that was exhilarating."

"Perhaps you should walk the rest of the way."

"Why, sir, I am in complete control — just keep hold of my bridle for a moment while I catch my breath. That's a good lad."

They crossed High Street at a more sedate pace, where a moon only slightly over half full hung over the castle. Then they were heading down Broad, on the home stretch, with warmth, comfort, and a meal waiting for them at the house on Bell Lane. Stephen tried to wiggle his missing toes to still an itch that wasn't there, thinking with anticipation of cabbage soup. Poor Bernard wouldn't be eating anything tonight, and he wondered about the man's mother in that cold cottage with only the cow for company now. The world was full of hardship.

The gate at the inn was shut but not barred, and all Stephen had to do was push it open with a foot. He hopped off to bar it, then led the mare back to the stable yard, where Gilbert had already dismounted and was stretching off the kinks from their little ride.

"I'll take care of the animals," Stephen said. Gilbert was as likely to feed a horse's ass as its head.

"Thank you," Gilbert said and tottered toward the house. "I've had enough of mules. What have I ever done that he should be so disobedient?"

"You ride him," Stephen said.

"Isn't that what you're supposed to do with mules?"

"Not the way you do it."

"Well," Gilbert harumphed, drawing himself up to his full height, which wasn't very impressive, since he stood only as tall as Stephen's chin. "I'll have you know I'm an excellent rider of mules. That mule is eccentric." He continued into the house.

Stephen had just fed the horse and mule when he heard two men shouting at each other in the street before the inn.

Abruptly the argument broke off. Stephen thought the matter concluded. He reached for a pitchfork to put down hay when he heard a frantic voice call: "Come out! Out! Felony!"

The hair on his neck tingled. It was the distinctive call of the hue and cry, summoning all within hearing because a crime had been committed.

Stephen threw up the bar on the gate, and ran into the street. Other men were coming out of their houses along Bell Lane to see what was the matter, while a group had collected in a knot before an alleyway across the way. Stephen crossed to them, since that seemed to be where the crime had taken place.

A few people recognized him and made way so he could pass to the center, where a body sprawled on the ground face down. The dagger scabbard on the body's left hip was empty. The dagger that should have been in it protruded from the back to the left of the spine, exactly where a man's heart should be. Stephen knelt and shook the man's shoulder. He did not respond. Stephen felt the man's neck for a pulse. There was none.

"A candle!" Stephen barked. "Fetch me a candle."

One of the neighbors procured a candle from his house and came forward, shielding the little flame with a palm from the night breeze.

Stephen held the candle close to the dead man's face, which was veiled by a curtain of hair. Stephen pulled the hair aside.

It was Ancelin Baynard.

Chapter 13

The coroner's inquest convened on Monday afternoon in the council room of the town's guild hall.

As the presiding officer, Stephen sat at the end of the hall by the big fireplace, occupying the high-backed chief alderman's chair with its pillowed seat. Before him the twelve jurors sat on benches facing each other. The brown, burnished wood of the floors, walls and supporting pillars added to a sense of gloom that pervaded the hall, unrelieved by the glow from the fire or the candles on Gilbert's writing table.

The hall was packed with spectators. Normally, the jurors investigated the circumstances of the death and reported them at the inquest. But a fierce storm had blown up during the night that made that job difficult. The witnesses had come to report to the assembled jury. Because Baynard had been well known, if not well liked, a large number of citizens had shown up too, and the din of conversation almost made Stephen's teeth rattle.

"Quiet down out there," Stephen called out as the jurors finally settled onto their benches. "We've work to do and we can't do it with all that noise."

When the clamor died down, he turned to Gilbert. "Call the first case."

Gilbert intoned first in French and then in English, "Hear ye, hear ye, we are here to consider the unrightful death of Bernard Gilley, the honorable deputy coroner Stephen Attebrook presiding,"

Since Stephen and Gilbert had already investigated Gilley's death and had taken statements from the witnesses, Gilbert presented the report to the jurors for their judgment.

The crowd had not come to hear about Gilley and did not care about the death of a mad man. Laughter broke out when Gilbert recounted Gilley's capering and singing, which led to his fatal plunge. A wave of conversation grew.

"If there isn't immediate silence, I'll have the hall cleared," Stephen snapped, "and you won't get to hear what you came for."

The threat brought swift compliance, and in the ensuring silence, the panel made short work of the case, finding that Gilley's death was an accident and assessing the bundle of roof thatch on which he stumbled at a quarter penny.

Gilley's mother collapsed at the verdict. For a moment Stephen was impatient with her grief, but then he thought about his own loss and how difficult it was to let it go. He had only lost a wife, who in theory was replaceable. This woman had lost a son who was not.

Stephen handed Gilbert a quarter penny, which he had received from the bailiff of her hundred, who were responsible for the fine. "Here is the amount in fine," he said. "Mistress Gilley, you have my profound sympathy and that, I'm sure, of all those who are assembled here. Do you have friends who can care for you in your distress?"

Mistress Gilley did not respond. Two neighbor women took her arms and led her through the crowd to the main doors, which opened to admit steel gray light and a chill wet blast of wind that sent the spectators crouching and threatened to extinguish the candles. Then the doors closed and the hall fell dark again.

"Next case," Stephen said.

"The matter of the unrightful death of Ancelin Baynard," Gilbert announced.

The crowd stirred in anticipation, but immediately fell silent as Stephen leaned forward with a thunderous scowl.

"Who will be the first witness?" Stephen said.

A little bald man in the front row raised his hand. "Your honor, if you could hear my mother first, it would be a great kindness. She's tired from the standing."

"Bring her forward."

The little bald man led out an old woman.

"Your name?" Stephen asked.

The woman squinted in his direction, then looked around. She whispered, "What was that, Alric?" Her voice was thin and reedy.

"He wants to know your name, mum."

"Well, why don't you go ahead and tell him. It's rude not to introduce a person."

"Her name is Jermina," the bald man said.

"Jermina," Stephen said, "please tell us what you know about the death of Ancelin Baynard."

"What did he say?" Jermina said.

"He wants to know what happened, mum. Go ahead, tell him, just like you told us."

"Well, then," Jermina said in a voice so thin it was almost a hiss. "I couldn't sleep. I often have trouble sleeping, you know. So when I do, I just get up, and sometimes that helps. I was sitting up by the window —"

"She has the front room overlooking the street," Alric interjected.

"— looking at the stars and these men began shouting. A terrible argument it was. They said horrible things to each other, foul things. I've never heard two men use such words in my house."

"They weren't in the house, mother," Alric said.

"It doesn't matter. I was in the house and I could hear them."

"What men were they?" Stephen asked.

"Oh, that man."

"What man?"

"That awful man. That man who died, and another."

"Can you give me his name?"

"I thought I'd already done so."

"I didn't hear it."

"Oh. Why, that fellow Baynard. He owes my Alric money. Hasn't paid. Said he won't until he gets satisfaction. Nasty man. You must know him. Everyone does."

"We've met. Who was the other man?"

"What other man?"

"The man with whom Master Baynard was arguing."

"I don't know."

"What did they say?" Stephen asked, straining to contain his exasperation.

"I'll not repeat such words."

"Not the curses. What were they arguing about?"

"It had to do with a woman. He had come to visit a woman."

"Who had come? Baynard?"

"Oh, no, young man, although I daresay he has a mistress or two tucked in around town. All his sort do. No, it was the other fellow."

"The young man has a mistress?"

"No, that Baynard man. Horrible man."

"Could you identify the younger man?"

"Oh, no. I never saw his face."

"Did you see the killing?"

"Certainly not."

Stephen resisted the urge to drum his fingers on the arm rests. "Thank you, mother. That has been very helpful. Alric, do you have anything to add?"

"No, your honor. We sleep at the back of the house. We heard nothing untoward."

Stephen glared at the crowd. "Is there anyone else who can shed light on this matter?"

Over the next hour a number of people living on Bell Lane came forward to tell their stories. They had heard the altercation too, but had not seen it. None could identify the killer.

After the last such witness, there was a long pause. Stephen was about to adjourn the matter so the jurors could canvas the neighborhood, in case there was a witness who had not come today because of the rain. Then a gaunt woman stepped from the crowd. She was somewhere close to fifty. Her face was a study in vertical lines with deep clefts at the corners of her eyes and mouth which gave her face a boxy appearance. She dressed all in black and wore a bronze cross on a heavy chain round her neck.

Although she lived alone across the street from the Broken Shield, Stephen struggled to recall her name. Then it popped into his head: Felicitas Bartelot.

"Widow Bartelot," Stephen said. "You know something of this?"

"I do indeed," Mistress Bartelot said in a voice severe and formal. "For I saw it happen."

Stephen was inclined to be skeptical, given what he had heard so far.

"Go on," he said.

"Or I should say, I saw its aftermath," Mistress Bartelot said primly.

"You did not see the blow struck," Stephen murmured.

"I did not. Like the others who testified today, I heard the shouting. Unlike some of them, I opened my window to see what was the matter, and I had a good view of things, for the men were at the mouth of the alley that runs beside my house, so it was an easy thing to peer out and see them."

"What did you see?"

"I saw a man who had just fallen lying on the ground and another kneeling over him. I did not see them well, for it was dark in the alley."

"So you did not see the killer's face?"

"To the contrary. I saw it quite plainly. Not then, but a moment later, when he stepped from the corpse and into the moonlight. Yes, I saw his face then."

"Who was it? Did you know him?"

"I knew him. So do many of the people in this room. For he is here, undoubtedly pretending innocence, thinking that he was not seen, that he has done his murder in secret."

For a moment, there was a silence so profound that Stephen could hear droplets from a leak in the roof splash into a puddle behind him. Then a great shout, as if from a single voice, bellowed from the crowd as everyone began talking at once.

Stephen bellowed for silence, and when it finally arrived, he asked Mistress Bartelot, "Who is that man?"

"There he is," she said. "That little man, there."

In the gloom, Stephen could not make out to whom Mistress Bartelot pointed. But there was a sudden commotion in the crowd, accompanied by shrieks and screams, and much shouting. Stephen swept off his chair. When he had forced his way through the press, Stephen found two burly men had hold of a small man by the arms. His head hung down so Stephen could not immediately tell who it was. Then the little man raised his head. His eyes were wild with fear.

It was Peter Bromptone.

Chapter 14

"It wasn't me," Peter said desperately but firmly. "We argued, but I swear, I didn't kill him. He was alive when I left him."

Stephen regarded him with a coldness partly tinged with dismay. He'd rather liked Peter. He had seemed decent and not the sort to resort to violence, but you could never tell about a man. "But you were seen standing over him."

"I won't deny it. I turned away. Then I heard a commotion. I looked around and saw him fall. But when I reached him, he was already dead."

"And you saw no one else."

After a long pause, Peter said, "No."

By this time, the town bailiff had come up with two of his men to formally arrest Peter. Stephen glanced at them, and said to Peter, "A fine story. Fortunately, it's not up to me to judge its truthfulness. Others will have that duty. It's enough to find that there is a reasonable suspicion you may have done murder. That's all we are charged here to do. And I think we have more than enough for that. You are attached to appear before the crown court. Until then you can make the acquaintance of the gaol. The bailiff can have you now."

As Gilbert scribbled out the reports of the session, the crowd broke up and began streaming out the front doors into the drizzly afternoon.

Stephen sat in his chair watching the people shuffle out, feeling glum.

"Why the long face?" Gilbert asked as he refreshed the quill in the ink pot. "Edith has planned a grand supper for us tonight. Roast beef, of the finest kind. How I love a good roast beef. Oh, and by the way, Jennie came while you were having your heart to heart with young Bromptone. She said that the burning of the latrine was completed. Went quite without a hitch."

"Even with the rain?" Stephen asked, still anxious that the body might have been detected.

"It's a miracle what man can do with dry branches and a little oil."

"At least we don't have to worry about that."

"One hopes not. Too bad about young Bromptone. I didn't know him well, but he never seemed the sort for killing anyone, let alone his master. Terrible thing, killing a master."

"He'll hang for it," Stephen said, "when the crown judge gets here. Nobody will tolerate treason like that."

"Which will be next week, I believe. The judge is in Hereford now and should wrap up court there by Friday. Edith had a note by the wagon post that his clerks wished to engage rooms starting Saturday night for a week."

Stephen smiled thinly. "We could have our hanging by next Thursday, then."

"I'd say so. Always nice to have a hanging on a market day. It's good for business."

"Good for business … I hadn't thought of that."

"Of course not, you're gentry."

"Used to be," Stephen said sourly.

"Something will turn up, God willing," Gilbert said. "Don't give up hope."

"I've used up my chits with God."

"Hush, lad, some priest will overhear you, or that magpie Mistress Bartelot, who wears her religion on her sleeve. Then God knows what penance you'll have to do for loose talk."

"I rather thought she wore her religion round her neck," Stephen said.

"Round her neck, indeed," Gilbert chuckled. He put up his pen and blew on the writing to dry the ink. "There. Finished. We can go now. Perhaps supper will be ready."

"I could use a drink. Some Gascon wine."

"Hum, Gascon wine. That'll cost you."

"I expected no less, you robber."

"Not me. That's my Edith. Always counting every penny."

"With you looking over her shoulder."

"Not all the time. She's very dependable." Gilbert rolled up the parchment and tied it with a ribbon.

A figure emerged from the gloom by the door. The scrape of her footfalls across the hall echoed in its emptiness. Stephen saw it was Amicia Bromptone. He wondered with a guilty pang how much she had heard.

"Next Thursday," she said heavily, indicating she must have heard quite a lot. "He has just over a week. How much justice will he get from the king's judge, when he and his father back the barons against the king? Precious little."

"On facts as the ones we have heard today, no man would get an acquittal," Stephen said.

"They are not the whole facts."

"How do you know?" Stephen asked. "Were you there?"

"I know my Peter! He's quick with his tongue but not with a knife. He couldn't have done this."

"The evidence suggests otherwise. It won't be the first time an apprentice killed his master."

"What do you know about the life of an apprentice? What do you know about the torment it can be?"

"I know well enough," Stephen said. "My father put me out to work for a lawyer in London who was every bit as hard a master as Baynard."

Gilbert burst out, "So we may take it that you ran too?"

Stephen glared at him.

Stephen went on, "The facts are, Peter could easily have killed Baynard. He surely had reason to."

"Reason! What reason!" Amicia cried.

"You," Stephen said. "The argument the witnesses recalled was about you. Undoubtedly, Baynard spied Peter going out at night without permission. He deduced Peter was on his way to you. He caught up and forbade Peter to see you, as a master has every right to do. Peter, of course, refused to obey in his usual temperate way. It's easy to see how such an argument could lead to blows."

"You don't know this!" Amicia gasped.

"All it takes it is to put the question to Peter. I doubt he'll deny that he was coming to see you. No one will believe if he denies it anyway, once people learn where you're staying." Stephen shrugged. "It is but a small leap to conclude that his confrontation with Baynard led to murder. Men killing over women is a common thing."

Amicia clasped her hands as if in prayer. "What can I do to save him?" She asked plaintively.

"Perhaps you'd be well advised to hire a lawyer," Gilbert said. "Sometimes the judge will allow a lawyer to speak for the accused. It's rare, but it has happened."

"I have nothing to pay a lawyer," Amicia said. "Or anyone else to find the truth." She paused and added in a subdued tone, "At least in money."

Stephen looked at her sharply.

When he remained silent, she added, "Is there no room in your heart for even the slightest doubt of his guilt?"

"Doubt," Stephen mused as if to himself. "Doubt. I have plenty of doubt. Gilbert would say my greatest weakness is too much doubt."

"Quite right," Gilbert said.

"But not about this?" Amicia asked.

"The Widow Bartelot saw him over the body," Stephen said. "He had motive, means, and opportunity."

Amicia closed her eyes in pain. "I shall have to find another, then."

She turned to go.

"Wait," Stephen said.

Amicia turned back to see what he wanted.

"Let me talk to Peter first."

She looked relieved and anxious at the same time.

Stephen said, "As to payment, if it becomes necessary, what you offer is too high. We will make some other arrangement."

Amicia's hands flew to her mouth. She was about to babble something, thanks or an excuse perhaps, but Stephen raised a hand to stop her. "Go now," he said. "Edith will be wondering what happened to you, and I'm sure you have work to do."

After Amicia fled the hall, Gilbert said, "Well, well. I shall swoon."

"Shut up, you old fart."

Gilbert tugged Stephen's arm to force him to his feet. "Come on, you young fart. Supper will soon be on the table. Let's have that and then go see Peter."

"Baynard caught you on the way to see Amicia, didn't he, Peter," Stephen said.

Peter's mouth drooped. He nodded curtly.

"Without permission."

"Of course, without permission." Apprentices were not allowed out at night without their master's permission, although it wasn't unusual for them to sneak away for the pleasures of the evening. Masters knew they did so, and often chose to look away if no work was neglected. But if the master did not disregard such a breach of the rules and inflicted punishment, it could be harsh.

Stephen shook his head.

"It pleased him to deny me that small pleasure," Peter said bitterly.

"And you defied him."

"I intended to."

"As you always defied him."

"Only when my rights were at stake."

"And when he turned his back, you grabbed his dagger and stabbed him in the back."

"No!" Peter shot back. "I never did. I was across the street on the inn's doorstep when I heard the scuffle."

Stephen held Peter's eyes. Although those eyes were hot with emotion, they were steady. There wasn't a flicker of guilt in them he could see. "Scuffle?" he said softly. "You didn't describe it as a scuffle earlier."

Peter pressed his lips together and ran his fingers through his hair. "Well, scuffle may not be the right word. A scraping, like the sound that shoes make. Something that sounded like a thump. I think, but I'm not sure. It was so faint." His eyes traveled around the interior of the cell as if seeing something other than cold gray stones. "And a gasp, but that was faint too. It all happened so fast."

"And then what happened."

"I turned back and Baynard was on his knees. At first I thought he'd had a stroke. Then he fell forward as I rushed to him, and I saw the knife."

"You saw no one else."

Peter shook his head. "The street was deserted."

"Not a soul was about?"

"I saw no one."

"But what did you hear?"

Peter's face screwed up in an effort to dredge his memory. "I heard someone running."

"One person or two?"

"One person."

"In which direction?"

"Toward Mill Street."

"And you still saw no one."

"I didn't look. At that moment Mistress Bartelot raised the hue and cry."

"And you ran away."

"I was afraid."

"It makes you look guilty."

"I know. I couldn't help myself. I didn't have the courage to stay. I thought perhaps she didn't see me."

"And you came to the inquest."

"The entire household came. It would have looked suspicious if I hadn't. And . . . and . . . I had a note from Amicia that she would be there. I had to see her."

Stephen leaned forward, his elbows on his knees. He and Gilbert had the benefit of stools, but Peter sat cross legged on the floor before them. Stephen had placed his stool in the middle of the cell. Gilbert, however, had remained close to the door, in case the gaoler decided to eavesdrop.

Stephen ran over in his mind what Peter had said and all his impressions of Peter's behavior. A good liar deceives with more than words alone: the tone of voice, the cast of eye, a well-timed gesture — a harmony of effect coated the lie in the trappings of truth. If Peter was deceiving him, he was doing a good job. Everything he had said and how he had carried himself seemed truthful. In the end, however, Stephen wasn't sure that it really mattered.

Stephen delved into his belt pouch and removed a leaf of parchment, a little red clay ink bottle, and a wooden stylus. "I want you to write your father a letter," he said.

Peter looked at him in bewilderment. "Why?"

"What he decides to do determines how much I can help you."

Peter smoothed the parchment on his legs and reached for the ink bottle and stylus. He spun the stylus in his fingers for a moment, thinking. Stephen wondered if he would refuse. Then Peter nodded.

Stephen smiled. "Good. Take down exactly what I say."

Stephen and Gilbert passed the gaoler, a skinny man with a harelip who was peeling an apple with his knife.

"Get a confession?" the gaoler said.

"No," Stephen said.

"Got to beat them, that's how to do it," the gaoler cackled. "This jawing doesn't do no good. Never can break a man with words."

"A confession under torture is rarely useful," Gilbert said.

"Ah, you're the clerk who was a priest," the gaoler spat. "Course you'd say that. Mercy don't get you nowhere, father. Deal with his sort long enough and you'd know that."

"Make sure the boy isn't touched, or I'll show you the meaning of mercy," Gilbert snapped.

"Oh, you put me in fear, father," the gaoler cackled. "I'm in fear!"

They reached the castle gate, but could still hear the gaoler laughing to himself. "Works with witches!" the gaoler shouted.

"He'd sing a different song if it was him chained to the wall," Gilbert muttered. They paused to admit a couple of clerks who hurried by on some unfinished business at the end of the day. Gilbert went on, "You sure you want to do this?"

"You think it's wrong?"

"It's a damned strange price. You could lose your head collecting it."

"Maybe so," Stephen said. "Everybody has a price. This is mine. But whether the price is paid, I'll find the truth. And it will fall where it falls, for good or ill for Master Bromptone."

He pushed past Gilbert into the street.

"If you live," Gilbert said to his back.

Chapter 15

Stephen blew out the candle and sat on the edge of his bed. After having paid the stabling fee for his horses for the next three months, he'd used the last of the money from returning Bromptone to buy a feather mattress. This was the first night he'd had it on the bed, and he was looking forward to sinking into it. He hadn't had a feather mattress of his own since he left home many years ago.

He removed his boots and massaged his stump. It tingled under his fingers. There were knots in the muscles of his foot and he kneaded them out with his thumbs.

Then he sat for a moment before laying back, savoring the soft mattress. Straw mattresses sometimes felt as though you were sleeping on hard ground.

The inn below him was silent. Only the occasional thump and murmur of voices announced the retirement of the occupants. Sometimes about now an argument broke out among the guests who had to share a bed, as they negotiated rationing of the available space. But no such argument disturbed this night. There was a scurrying sound overhead: a mouse on its nightly patrol among the rafters. He became conscious that the patter of rain on the roof had stopped. And a silvery glow outlined the closed shutters of his window. The moon was out.

Seized by a sudden thought, Stephen padded to the window and threw open the shutters. Below, the yard, stables, and orchard lay before him in sharp relief in the lamplight of a three-quarters moon. The sky had largely cleared. Last night would have been illuminated not much differently than this.

Stephen retied his boots and stumped down the stairway in the dark, in such a hurry that he did not pause for his candle.

On the last flight, he met Gilbert and Edith on their way up. Gilbert had his arm around Edith's rather substantial waist.

"What's the emergency?" Gilbert said as Stephen blundered past with a hasty apology. "The house on fire?"

"Come on, I've had a thought."

"Lord, a soldier who thinks — that's unusual."

"There's not a moment to spare. The light may change."

"The light?" Gilbert asked. He was bewildered, but he handed his candle to Edith. "I'll see you in a bit, my little sweetmeat. It appears that duty calls. Keep the bed warm for me."

Edith grunted, whether from assent or displeasure it was impossible to say. She took the candle and continued upstairs.

Stephen and Gilbert went out into Bell Lane. Stephen stood at the doorstep and surveyed the street. The lane was so narrow and the inn so tall, as were the other houses on the south side, that the lane was in moonshadow. He looked to the right, toward Mistress Bartelot's house. A gap in the houses on the south side, like the peaks of mountains, allowed moonlight to fall at the mouth of the alley near the spot where Baynard had died, much as he remembered the moment when he had stood over Baynard's body.

Stephen crossed the lane to the head of the alley. Moonlight shone on the wall of Bartelot's house and partway down the alley. There was a waist-high pile of firewood in the alley. At the end was a tall fence. A man could climb over that fence, but he'd make a lot of noise leaping to the top and clambering over.

To the left at the mouth of the alley were two large barrels. A spout ran to them from the roof, where there was a gutter to collect rainwater. He looked into the barrels. They were full, their sides mossy. Some people collected water this way so they didn't have to go to the town well. He dipped a hand in the water and sipped. The water was fresh and sweet. It was only then that he noticed the barrels stood out far enough from the wall that a man might squeeze through the gap. He pondered this fact for a moment. It seemed an unlikely long shot. But then . . .

"Gilbert," Stephen said, "go back to our doorstep and watch the mouth of the alley."

Puzzled but unquestioning, Gilbert strode back to the inn's door. As he did so, Stephen stooped and wormed his way behind the barrels. It was a tight fit, but he made it.

"Now, come across the lane to the spot where Baynard was found and kneel facing Bartelot's house!" Stephen called.

"Where'd you go?"

"Never you mind. Just do it."

Stephen heard Gilbert's measured tread recross the lane. He dared a peek around a barrel and saw Gilbert at the death spot, settling to his knees. Stephen slipped backward, keeping the barrel between him and Gilbert. Ducking low, he scuttled westward down Bell Lane, keeping to the houses along the north wall. About forty yards from the alley, he reached Raven Lane. He ducked around the corner, then peered back to see what Gilbert was doing. Gilbert was standing at the mouth of the alley now, visible only as a silhouette. He was looking up and down Bell Lane.

"All right," Gilbert called out. "Stop playing games."

Stephen smiled and headed back up Bell Lane.

"What was that about?" Gilbert asked as he drew up.

"Did you see me?" Stephen asked.

"No. I thought I heard you running but I couldn't see you."

"Good." He quickly outlined what he'd done.

Gilbert understood at last. "So someone could have hidden in the alley, killed Baynard, and slipped away without Bromptone seeing."

"Yes."

"But that suggests that whoever killed him lay in wait." Gilbert motioned toward the alley. "In there."

"Which means that the killer lured him out. If we know how, perhaps we can tell who. The question is, who might know?"

"I'd talk to that thick-necked fellow Clement, or his widow. If anyone knows, they do."

Chapter 16

The cocks crowed as Tuesday morning threw melancholy gray light across the town.

Stephen rose and pushed open the shutters. Despite yesterday's rain, the air smelled foul from the burnt privy, which was still smoldering. A dog barked in the yard behind. The stable doors were open, which meant that Harry had already left for Broad Gate. It was getting late. He had better hurry, or the best part of the morning would be lost.

He washed in the basin beside the window, as he did every morning. The cool water stung his bare skin. He thought about Taresa as he washed. Sometimes she had washed him, drawing the soapy rag, the rinse, and then the towel slowly over his entire body. The memory filled him with sadness. More than six months had passed since her death, but his grief was still sharp.

He poured the wash water out the window, and got dressed. This was no ordinary day, and ordinary clothes would not do. He struggled into his best shirt and hose, then belted on his sword and picked up the spare blade and shield.

Gilbert met Stephen at the foot of the stairs. "You're going then," he said sourly.

"I am."

"Bromptone may kill you as soon as talk to you. You're a fool to take that risk."

"Fool enough for two men at least." Stephen smiled.

"Sure you don't want me to go with you?"

"Will Edith let you?"

"I'm the master of my ship. I don't have to explain anything to her."

"Well, I do. Mother would be most displeased with me if you came along. Anyway, if things go bad, I'll need someone good at fighting, not at spouting Latin. Now, if you could throw around an excommunication or two, that might be helpful. But you've been out of that line of work for some time."

Jennie emerged from the passage leading to the kitchen with a small sack, which she handed to Stephen. "There's a little extra for breakfast too."

Gilbert said, "Damn you, boy. You be careful." He added softly so the guests couldn't hear, "I didn't burn that latrine so you could go get your head hacked off."

"Speaking of the latrine, it's a good day to fill it in. It was stinking to high heaven this morning."

Jennie wrinkled her nose. "It is, dad. Can't you smell it?"

Gilbert looked aghast that conversation had turned to this topic, for Jennie had no idea of the unmentionable thing that lay in the pit. He sputtered to Stephen, "Go on, get out of here before I make you pay for your dinner."

Stephen said, "I'll see you at supper."

"You had better."

Stephen waved and went out the side door to the yard. He heard Jennie say, "What was that about?"

"Never you mind," Gilbert said.

Normally there was a groom on duty. But he was not in evidence, and Stephen saddled the stallion himself. The horse pulled away, kicked, snorted, and reared as Stephen tried to slip the bridle over his head so that Stephen was afraid the horse would crush him against the wall. Stephen threw a blanket over the horse's head, and talked quietly until the stallion calmed down. He gave the stallion a piece of an apple. After a while, the horse allowed him to put on the bridle.

Bell Lane was awake by the time he emerged from the yard. The old woman Jermina was sweeping off the stoop of the house across the street, while Alric, her son, raked bits of trash before the house, as it was every householder's responsibility to keep clean the stretch of street before their doorstep. The windows were already open on Alric's shop and a boy was visible inside cutting leather for a shoe. Behind him on shelves were rows and rows of wooden pattens — the carved forms of people's feet around which shoes were fitted to the proper size. They all waved as he went by. Next door, Mistress Bartelot sat at an upper window sipping a hot drink that emitted wafts of steam about her long face. Stephen had seen tombstones that were more cheerful. Nonetheless, courtesy required that he call a good day to her. She looked startled at the attention, jerked her head in what Stephen took to be a nod of greeting, and muttered something that might have been a reply, her fingers busy on her massive bronze cross.

Stephen reached Broad Street and turned north toward the top of the hill where traffic was heavy, both cart and foot. The stallion did not handle the congestion well, but by keeping to the margins, Stephen reached the top of Broad Street without trampling anyone.

At the top of the ridge, he glanced left for a view of the throng gathering for market day. High Street was filling with merchants and farmers clear to the castle gate. The spots for all the sellers had been marked off with stakes and ropes by the market bailiffs. Many of the sellers had booths — wood-frames with canvas stretched over them to make a little tent and trestle tables — set up in their assigned spaces. Others just backed in a cart or stretched a blanket on the ground.

Like everyone else, Stephen enjoyed market day. But today, its simple pleasures, the simmering sweet buns, the sausages and cheeses, the fresh baked breads, ale dispensed from a keg in the back of a wagon, the conversation, a game of dice on a blanket, were denied him. The business of death called instead.

Stephen crossed High and entered College Lane. St. Laurence's brown bulk loomed to the right, overwhelming the lane, which was just wide enough for two carts to pass each other.

Baynard house, lying before the little gate into Linney, looked even more mournful than when Stephen had seen it last. Not a window was open, which was unusual since the gray dawn had given way to a cheerful morning of bright sun and scattered clouds. On such a day, everyone was eager to throw open their windows and admit this glorious light. Everyone, it seemed, but the Baynards. Someone had nailed a big strip of black ribbon to the door frame, a sign the house was in mourning as if in warning for visitors to go away.

Stephen knocked on the door. The thuds of the knocker echoed up the empty lane. No one answered. He knocked again and waited. Still, no one came. He began to think the family wasn't at home.

He was about to turn away when the door opened a crack. "Yes?" It was Muryet, the butler.

"I'd like to see Clement," Stephen said.

"I'm afraid that's impossible."

"Why?"

"He is not at home." Muryet started to close the door. Stephen put his shoulder against the door panel.

"Where is he?"

The little man looked startled at this, but did not attempt to close the door any further. "None of your business." He called into the interior of the house, "Howard! Come quickly."

Within moments, a hulking man loomed behind the little one. "What's happening, sir?"

"This person is being rude. Please see him on his way."

"Gladly, sir." Howard pulled open the door. Stephen stepped back to avoid falling on his face. Howard reached for Stephen's lapel. Stephen grasped Howard's wrist before he achieved a grip and struck him sharply on the elbow with the other hand. Howard cried out and cradled his injured arm to his chest.

"If you want to keep the arm, go back inside," Stephen said. He returned his attention to the little man, whose shock at Stephen's treatment of Howard showed plainly on his face. Stephen said, "If he touches me, I'll have you both attached to answer for assaulting a crown officer. This is official business. Your name's Muryet, correct?"

The small man regarded Stephen haughtily, intimidated neither by Stephen's position nor the threat. "I am William Muryet."

"I understand you're the butler."

"That's correct."

"Do you live in this house?"

"I have rooms here."

"Were you on duty the night Master Baynard died?"

"What is this about?"

"Answer the question now, or answer it again before the jury."

"The inquest is closed. I was there. I saw it."

"I have opened it again."

Muryet said, "I was on duty."

"Why did Master Baynard leave the house after curfew?"

"I don't know."

The answer came too quickly. "I don't believe you."

The little man's mouth worked again. "He had a message."

"From whom?"

"I don't know."

"Who was the messenger?"

"There was no messenger that any of the household saw. There was a knock on the door. When I answered it, I found a note pinned to the door."

"What did it say?"

"It was addressed to the master and sealed. I am . . . was . . . not in the habit of reading his correspondence."

"You delivered it to Master Baynard, then?"

"Of course."

"What did he do with the note?"

"I have no idea."

There was something evasive in Muryet's eyes. "Baynard read the message?"

"Yes."

"In your presence."

Muryet nodded.

"What did Baynard do with the note after he read it?"

Muryet hesitated. "He put it on the table."

"The table in the hall?"

"No, he has a library. He does his work there."

"Well, then, it should still be there, shouldn't it?"

"I wouldn't know."

"Why?"

"I do not concern myself with the master's affairs."

"And you swear you did not read the note at any time either before or after your master's death?"

"Of course I did not read it."

Stephen said, "What did Baynard do after he put it down?"

"Put what down?"

"The note."

"He went out."

"Did he say where he was going?"

"No."

"Did he often just run off after dark without a word where he was going?"

Muryet said nothing.

"Wasn't his wife concerned? It's quite odd for a man to rush off like that after dark without a word to anyone."

Muryet hissed, "Listen, you. The master had his business. Sometimes it involved a young woman. He was a rich man and entitled. We never asked questions. No one ever asked questions. Hear?"

Stephen was taken aback. Had Baynard just gone out to see a woman? It was a reasonable explanation. He could have rushed out to see her and encountered Peter Bromptone by accident. Instead of a plot, it could just as easily have been coincidence.

Stephen was about to ask for the note, but his pause was all that Muryet needed to slam the door in his face. "Good day!" Muryet shouted through the door.

Stephen called his name and knocked, but no one came.

Arnold Bromptone descended the stairs of Wickley manor to where Stephen waited in the yard. He said, "You have nerve coming here."

"Ancelin Baynard is dead," Stephen said.

Bromptone managed to look convincingly surprised. "Of what? His bad temper?"

"I think you know."

"Are you accusing me?" Bromptone's face was thunderous.

Stephen handed him Peter's letter.

Bromptone paused before taking it, as if the parchment was poisoned.

"It's not a warrant, if that's what you're worried about," Stephen said.

Bromptone examined the wax for a seal, but there was none; it was just a plain daub of green wax. He broke the seal and read the letter, his expression growing more angry. He slapped the letter. "Peter is accused of the crime?" he sputtered. "What nonsense! He's not capable of this. The boy's headstrong, but he's run from fights ever since he was a child. He could talk a man to death, but stab him? No."

"Yet he was found over the body and he had reason. You know that such evidence is more than enough."

"Yet he says you will help."

"But he also says there will be a cost."

"And he says I'm to tell you the truth." Bromptone rolled up the letter and batted it against his palm. "It is a steep price."

"Nevertheless, that is it."

"You don't know what you're asking. There are things I cannot speak of, no matter the consequences."

Stephen shrugged. "It is your choice."

"They tell a story about William Marshal, the first earl of Pembroke. Perhaps you've heard it. His father joined the rebellion against King Stephen, taking a castle with him. The king, who already held William as a hostage, laid siege to the castle. The king brought forth the boy and said he would kill him if William's father would not surrender. His father replied that the king could do what he liked, for he had the hammer and the anvil to make another son. I have both the hammer and the anvil — and another son."

"Which, of course, is why you sent Peter to be a draper. I feel sorry for him. He will die at the end of a rope with a thief on one side of him and a pair of robbers on the other. I doubt that will do much good for your family reputation."

"Let me worry about my family's reputation. He should have thought of that when he married that girl."

"Were you going to find him a better marriage? Somehow I doubt it. You cast him away. He knew that. You cannot fault him for acting on it. Besides, he loves her."

Bromptone's expression seemed to soften for a moment. "Anyone would love a girl like that. You've seen her, haven't you?"

Stephen nodded. "She'd do even without a dowry."

"I doubt Peter got much for her, too. Is she a good girl?"

"She's trustworthy, I think, from what I've seen of her. And she loves him."

"Truly?"

"Yes. I'm afraid so."

"People who marry for love are fools."

"People who do not find love in marriage, even if they start without it, are fools."

"How would you know?"

"My mother told me that. Although how she could have loved my father, I don't know."

"You did not get along with him then, your father?"

"About as well as you and Peter."

"I, also. My father was a hard man."

"Men have to be hard, but even hard men can have pity. It is not a fault."

Bromptone looked Stephen in the eye. "I don't want him to die."

"Nor I."

Bromptone raised the letter. "This is his hand, but the words do not sound like him."

"I dictated the contents. Except the end. Those words are his."

Baynard nodded, his eyes focused on a distant spot beyond Stephen.

Stephen said, "Did you put him up to it?"

Bromptone looked wounded. "I swear, I didn't. Why would you suspect that?"

"There's a grudge between you and Baynard. Your son loves you, and wants to please you. He just isn't sure how." Bromptone watched him warily and said nothing. Stephen went on, "You're of Montfort's party. Peter followed you. Baynard is for the king. It isn't an honorable way to buy back a father's love, but it is one way."

"Do you really believe he would kill Baynard?"

"No, but I think you would."

"You shouldn't pry into such things," Bromptone said.

"Do you want to save him, or not?"

"Even if the road leads to me?"

"Yes."

There was a long pause. "He hasn't been a good son."

"He's still your blood and carries your name."

Bromptone's face was bleak. "So my wife claims." Bromptone walked away a pace and stared across the stone fence into the stubbled field beyond. "It's odd. He was the one I loved best as a child. But as he grew older, he never did as I expected. He wouldn't fight, he wouldn't enter the church. When I finally found a place for him after much searching, he ran from his master. He married a common girl of no account without my leave." Bromptone turned back. "You say you don't believe he's guilty?"

Stephen ignored the question. "What more was there between you and Baynard?"

Bromptone sighed. "He was the king's master spy in this county. It was his task to ferret out all the supporters of the barons and to report them. At first we thought that was all. But then a few of our people started turning up dead, couriers and spies of our own, mostly. They were common people and we put the misfortune off to accident and paid little notice. But then two from the gentry were killed — one in

Shrewsbury and a second in Hereford — both knifed in the street at night. It was too much to suspect happenstance."

"So you ordered him killed."

"No! We only thought to send him a warning."

"Is that why you tried to kill me?"

"It wasn't my doing."

"Fitzsimmons?"

Bromptone nodded.

"But you concurred."

Bromptone nodded again.

"Because you thought I was one of Baynard's spies."

"Yes."

"I wasn't, and am not a king's spy."

"Why shouldn't we think so? You're Shelburgh's cousin, Sir Geoffrey's man and you came from Baynard."

Stephen smiled humorlessly. His cousin, the earl, was a king's man. "You failed to kill me, so you went to the source of the trouble."

Bromptone shook his head.

"If not you and not Peter, you'll have to tell me what I need to know if you want to save him."

Bromptone still stood mute.

Stephen said: "If not you, then it must have been Fitzsimmons."

"I don't know!" Bromptone gasped as if in pain.

"But you suspect," Stephen said remorselessly.

"I can't speak of it!"

"Why not?"

Bromptone's mouth worked soundlessly. He seemed to come to a decision. He said, "Nigel is . . . rather more than Baynard's counterpart. I don't know all he does."

"Baynard's counterpart . . . you mean . . ."

"He is the chief spy for Montfort in all of England, not merely this place," Bromptone said heavily. He added, "There's one thing you should know."

Lost in thought, Stephen was a moment responding. "What?"

"Nigel means to see you dead. It's gone beyond our game with the king's party. For him the grudge with you has become personal."

"How have I offended him?" Stephen asked, taken aback.

"One of those you killed on the road was his nephew, a boy he loved and fostered. It's feud now."

Stephen took a slow breath. Feud was a weighty and frightening thing. It was more than just a fight between individuals; it was family against family, and Stephen was not sure whether he could call on his for support. But most importantly, it meant Fitzsimmons felt honor-bound to take revenge, no matter the cost, no matter how long it took.

There was only one thing to do. Stephen threw one of his gloves on the ground at Bromptone's feet. He hated to do it, but it was the only way he could think of to end the game quickly. Stephen said, "Tell him to come for me himself, if he has the courage, rather than send his lackeys in the night."

Bromptone coolly regarded the glove. Then he picked it up. "When and where?" he asked flatly.

"Friday at terce, before Ludford parish church. It's a nice spot, good for horses — and he can be planted in the graveyard right after I kill him."

"It may be the other way around," Bromptone said softly. "He's the most formidable fighter I've ever seen."

"Well, then, let him come and prove it."

Chapter 17

"You're not going, then?" Edith asked, of Baynard's funeral mass. St. Laurence's bell could be heard announcing the start of it.

It was Wednesday, three days after Baynard's death and getting late for a funeral this time of year. Much more of an interval and the body would be too ripe for anyone to stand. The delay was to allow word to go out to the surrounding country side and friends from some distance to come to pay their respects.

"No," Stephen said, looking up from the stick he had been pretending to whittle. It seemed an interesting way to while away the time, but he wondered how Harry managed to turn a useless piece of wood into something pretty without cutting off a finger. "I don't think so. It isn't fit to mourn the death of a man you did not like."

"Like has nothing to do with it. He had a soul and it deserves a decent send off regardless of your opinion," she said. "It's the least you can do."

"I'll come up later, for the wake."

Edith pouted. "Is all you care about food and drink?" Her foot tapped the floor as her mind searched for other arguments. "Don't you realize that everyone who is anyone in town will be there?"

"So that's why you're going."

"We go to mourn a death, surely. But everyone who is anyone in town will be there. In a small town such as this, it's a good idea to see and be seen. Sad as they are, funerals are a place to renew old acquaintances and make new ones. Let people know you're not the ogre you seem to be."

"I'm an ogre?"

"Going around with that scowl all the time, people are beginning to think so. And you more than anyone needs to develop your prospects. They are quite low now and sinking."

"She's right about that," Gilbert said from the stairs.

"Right about what?" Stephen asked. "That I'm an ogre?"

"Not an ogre, but ogrish. At any rate, I was speaking of prospects."

"And I thought you were my friend," Stephen said. "I like your hat, by the way." It was in fact a rather ridiculous hat, massive and floppy, and seemed about to slide off Gilbert's head.

"Why thank you, but I know you don't mean it." Gilbert offered Edith his arm. "It's getting late, dear. We'll have to stand at the back if we dally much longer."

Edith took his arm but remained facing Stephen. "I insist you come."

"Nonetheless, I'll stay and keep Jennie company. She may need help if a customer gets out of hand." He saw her standing at the bar, a rag in hand, and winked at her. She blushed in return.

"You'll do nothing of the kind," Edith said, tugging his arm. "You're coming with us."

With Edith on one arm and Gilbert on the other, Stephen had little choice but to go along unless he wanted a physical struggle.

"You're as bothersome as my mother," he said.

"You are badly in need of a mother, if you ask me," Edith said as they descended into the street. "Since she is not here, I shall have to do."

Broad Street was full of foot traffic marching up the hill toward the church, its brownstone bell tower visible ahead over the rooftops. Good days were exchanged as they proceeded up Broad Street, for Gilbert and Edith knew everyone and were known by them.

At the entrance to St. Laurence's, Harry sat on one side of the churchyard gate. His plank leaned against the wall and he had his begging bowl on the ground before him. On the other side of the gate, stood another beggar, whom Stephen recognized as Fray, a broad-shouldered man with a black beard that resembled a ragged banner hanging to belt level.

Edith and Gilbert swept by with a brisk good morning, Harry.

"Yer looking well, Lady Edith!" Harry shouted at their backs. "Nice gown!"

Stephen stopped and bent over Harry's bowl. He counted three quarter pennies with his finger, enough for three loaves of bread. Not bad for a single morning's work. But he said, "Slim pickings this morning, Harry?"

"I'd do better if you'd get out of the way," Harry said.

Stephen stepped back. "Pardon me. I wouldn't want to interfere."

"That's better." Harry held his hands out to a passing couple who ignored him, except their young son who tried to kick over the bowl. Harry was too quick for that, though, and batted the boy's leg aside. "Get on, you!" he snapped. The boy danced after his parents.

Stephen leaned against the wall a short distance from Harry. A glance over his shoulder told him that Gilbert and, more importantly, Edith had found someone to talk to just outside the doors of the church, and had forgotten about him. As he watched, they went inside.

"So, Harry," Stephen said, "am I an ogre?"

"You ain't been the easiest person to be around these last few days. What's the matter, Baynard not pay all you're owed?"

"It's not that."

"And it's damned annoying the way you pound that post in the yard. All that racket, it could make a person's teeth fall out."

Stephen had been practicing with a wooden sword against a post in the yard. "Edith complained about that yesterday, too."

"Then why didn't you stop?"

"I need the exercise."

Harry shook his head at the marvel that someone had defied Edith, so far at least, and for such a thin reason. "What are you planning?"

"Me? Nothing."

"Something's up. I heard tell that Prince Edward has put out a call for troops. There's talk of an invasion of Wales next spring. You getting ready for it?"

"Is there?" Stephen said with some interest. "What else have you heard?"

"I'm not free with my talk, like some people in this town."

"Coming from you, I know it means you're not talking about keeping confidences."

Harry rattled the coins in his bowl. "Course it doesn't."

"I don't know."

"It's about Baynard."

Stephen prodded his purse with his fingertips, feeling its lack of weight. He dropped a farthing in Harry's bowl. "All right."

"That's it? This could be important. It could reveal all to you, the one thread you've missed that binds the whole."

"I doubt that."

Harry held up the farthing. "This looks counterfeit to me."

Stephen took it from him and gestured as if he planned to toss it across the path. "I'll let Fray have it then."

"No, don't do that. He'll just spend it on drink."

"While you won't."

"I've loftier ambitions than a night of drunken revelry." He held out the bowl. "Here, put it here, and I'll part with my secret."

Stephen returned the fragment of coin to the bowl.

Harry motioned for him to lean closer. "I can't just shout this out, you know." As Stephen bent down, he said, "Lucy Wattepas paused to talk with that fat lawyer de Kersey here at the gate as they were going in." He paused.

"So?" Stephen said.

"She asked him if he knew what was in the will."

"Did he?"

"He ought to. He wrote it."

"How do you know?"

"He must have. He's the only lawyer in town and he knew what was in it."

"All right then. On with it. Edith will be out here in a moment to drag me in."

"Can't have that. You'd defile the place with your presence. Anyway, he said he did. She asked if there was provision for the Palmer's Guild, and he said there was. He added a few other things about the will that I don't remember. Then he said one curious thing. He said Baynard had left five pounds to the Hytone woman and another five to her daughter for a dowry. He could not imagine why and he asked her if she knew." Harry grinned, revealing surprisingly straight and healthy teeth.

"Did she?"

"If she did, she wasn't letting on. But she's a canny bitch. I bet she knows. The news made her swell up like a fighting cock. Only the best gossip makes people react like that."

"And they said all of this in front of you."

"Not in front, exactly, but on the other side of yonder wall. As you know, I'm so short that I don't stick up. Besides, folk like that don't even notice folk like me."

Stephen frowned and stood up. "What's so important about this?"

Harry grinned with a trace of malice. "You don't know who I'm talking about?"

"Not a clue."

"Mistress Hytone runs a tavern off the road to Richards Castle, you dolt. You know, some people have questioned your intelligence, but I've always defended you. I wonder if I should do so from now on."

Stephen stood over Harry. Five pounds was about half what some lesser manors earned in a year. He said, "Five pounds each. That's a lot of money."

"Yeah. I could retire on five pounds," Harry said. "But you, you'd waste it on a horse, or something frivolous like that."

Stephen nodded. "They must have been lovers."

"Who, Baynard and the girl?" Harry said.

"No, Baynard and Johanna."

"That's just a wild guess. Could have easily been the girl."

"Then he wouldn't have given anything to the mother. Besides, I saw Pris meeting Patrick Carter's son, Edgar, the other day."

"Sheer speculation." Harry rattled the coins in his bowl. "I've another bit of gossip for you, if you're interested."

"This one wasn't worth a farthing."

"You are a man lacking in imagination."

Stephen said nothing.

Finally, Harry said, "All right. I saw Edgar and his mum Monday morning at Broad Gate."

"So?"

"So they were leaving the town at first light, not coming in."

Stephen tapped his foot, exasperated. "Harry, you try my patience. It's hardly even interesting, let alone helpful."

Harry shrugged. "All right then, go about your business, but stop bothering me so I can go about mine."

Stephen tossed a half penny into the bowl. "For your trouble."

"You're too kind, governor, too kind. If only all were generous as you, I'd be able to afford a decent pair of shoes."

"Whatever would you do with a pair of shoes? Wear them on your ears?"

"I'll need shoes after I buy myself some legs!" Harry hooted.

Chapter 18

Stephen went up College Lane to the wake. He had not been invited, but he didn't think he'd be questioned in the press.

A group of apprentice-aged boys and servant girls blocked the doorway. A boy came out with a small keg on his shoulder to the acclaim of those clustered about the stoop. The assembly, among whom doubtless were the servants charged with regulating entry, followed the keg-wielder away from the doorway, and Stephen took advantage of the distraction to slip into the hall.

Chairs and benches were arranged before the two enormous fireplaces to catch the best of the blazes. A band of musicians bravely plucked and fluted away by the biggest fireplace, the music unheeded by anyone and almost submerged in the hubbub. A long table laden with food, including a pig complete with its head and feet, occupied the center of the hall, while barrels of wine and ale stood against the left wall. The windows were tall, and mottled glass in the panes threw a greenish hue over everything.

Stephen scanned the crowd for the butler, Muryet, and Clement

He didn't see them, but there were so many people that he could easily have missed them.

He spotted the Widow Baynard in the master's high-backed chair surrounded by a cluster of matrons. Stephen would sooner approach the king than brave that formidable court and make what the widow and her friends must think was a strange request coming from the likes of him.

As he plotted how to approach her, he wandered over to the food-laden table. He washed his hands in the bowl set out for that purpose, and as he dried his hands, Gilbert and Edith appeared at his elbow. Gilbert's trencher already held a litter of bones.

"They have these little partridges that are excellent," Gilbert said. "Cooked in a lemon and pepper sauce. There, right behind the pig."

Stephen looked at the bones. "How many have you had?"

"Only three," Gilbert said defensively.

"Tell the truth."

"Well, I have. And if you want a partridge, you better move fast. There won't be any left soon."

"At the rate you're going, I'm not surprised. And you've only just got here."

Edith laughed. "I told him that if he didn't slow down, he'd be swallowing those birds whole!"

Gilbert looked miffed.

Stephen filled a trencher. He said, "Gilbert, you know the Widow Baynard, don't you?"

"We've met," Gilbert said. "But the Baynards aren't the sort to have much to do with innkeepers."

"I'm told Baynard had a library."

Gilbert brightened. "I've heard that too."

"Now that we're here, it would be interesting to have a look at it, don't you think?"

"Why, yes! Yes! What a fine idea. I didn't know you had an interest in books."

"I am a connoisseur of books."

"I've never seen you read a book."

"If I had a book, I'd read it. But I'm too poor."

Gilbert confided, "I have three!"

Stephen was surprised. "You don't say. I didn't know that."

"One's a Bible," he said with pride.

"How did you get hold of a Bible?"

Gilbert was suddenly evasive. Bibles cost a fortune and there weren't many outside abbeys. Edith looked at him sharply.

Stephen saw this was a question better left unanswered. "Well, you'll have to let me read it sometime."

"It'll do you good," Edith said.

"I wonder how we could get a peek at Baynard's library?" Stephen mused after a bite of pork.

"We shall have to ask the widow! That's what we'll do. Ask her. I'm sure she won't mind. What do you think, Edith?"

Edith looked skeptical. But she said, "I suppose you can."

"Right, then." He regarded his trencher. "Now? You want to go now?"

"Why not?" Stephen said. He'd finished his meal. It had been very good. He could do for more, but now that he had a plan, he was eager to get on with it.

"Oh, all right." Gilbert handed his trencher to Edith and moved through the crowd to the benches and chairs before the main fireplace, where the widow had established her court.

Edith put a slice of roasted peach in her mouth. She asked off-handedly, "Why didn't you just ask the widow yourself?"

Stephen felt himself start to blush. She at least had seen through him, if Gilbert had not. "The request would have been odd coming from me, and I don't want to draw attention to my interest."

"Why not?"

"There may be something in there of use in the case of Baynard's murder. Something others might be concerned that I not acquire."

"Why not just demand to search for it?"

"It's not really an official inquiry."

"We're not going to get in trouble for this, are we?"

"Not unless we're caught."

"Hmmph," Edith grunted.

Gilbert came back, beaming and rubbing his hands together. In his excitement about inspecting the library he had forgotten about his trencher. "Are you ready? Let's not dally!"

They met a servant at the foot of the stairs. They had to climb to the upper floors in full view of those in the hall, and Stephen worried that Muryet or Clement might spot him. Gilbert, who was right behind him, thought Stephen was looking at the widow in her circle before the fireplace. She was laughing and seemed to be enjoying herself.

Gilbert said, "For some women, widowhood is a release, not a time of grief."

"What's that?" Stephen asked.

Gilbert nodded to the Widow Baynard. "Some women are happier with their husbands dead than alive."

"You can't understand that because you're a man," Edith said.

"Are you unhappy, my dear?"

"I could be happier."

"Oh, dear. What can I do to assure your bliss?"

"You could listen better."

Stephen, who could recall only one instance when people didn't leap to obey when Edith commanded, said. "Let's get off the stairs." He took the remaining steps two at a time until he was out of sight of the floor below. He breathed a little easier now he couldn't be seen. But it transpired that they had to make one more exposed passage, the walkway above the hall to the front of the house. Stephen wished they could make the passage quickly, but the boy wasn't in any hurry.

The servant opened the door of a room which overlooked the hall below, and stood back. "The library, sirs, mistress," he said.

Stephen went in, followed by Gilbert and Edith. It was a small room, no more than eight feet wide by ten feet long. There was a window on the far wall which gave a view of the street. A window on the right, the south side of the house, opened to the space between this house and the neighbors. The shutters of both had been thrown back, which rendered the room bright and sunny, good for writing and reading. A set of shelves stood along the left wall, which held perhaps twenty books. Gilbert gasped at the sight of them.

"Good lord, what riches!" he said. "What riches indeed!"

He reverently took one of the books, bound in blue leather, and sank into the cushioned chair before a large writing table.

Stephen turned to the servant, who had remained in the doorway. The boy lingered there, as if he intended to watch them. Stephen couldn't have that. He said in his most bored tone, "Would you be so kind as to fetch us wine?"

"Of course, sir," the boy said.

"Thank you so much."

The boy turned back toward the stairway. Stephen closed the door. "Edith," he said, "will you keep a lookout?"

Edith looked startled, but nodded and positioned herself with an ear by the door so she could hear anyone approach.

Stephen hoped the boy would be in no more hurry to carry out that chore than he had been to lead them here. But even so, Stephen wouldn't have much time to search until the boy came back. As he surveyed the room, his dismay grew. It was barren except for the books, the writing desk, the cushioned chair and a stool. There was no box for documents, nor any indication of any place they might be kept — no cabinet, no hide-hole, no cupboard. Had Muryet been wrong? Stephen couldn't believe he had been — unless someone had removed the documents.

In his worry, Stephen inspected the most conspicuous piece of furniture of the room, the writing table. The top, like many such tables, lay at a slant to facilitate writing. He said, "Gilbert, move your elbow for me."

Gilbert blinked, shifted his position, and kept reading.

Stephen smiled. Below the front lip of the slanted top was the tooled mouth of a bronze keyhole. He jimmied the writing surface. It wiggled slightly but did not come up. It was locked. He thumped the top and sides, which gave back a hollow thunk. There was a document box and the desk was it.

"Do you know anything about lock picking?" Stephen asked Gilbert.

Gilbert said, "What do you take me for?"

Stephen drew his dagger and inserted the point between the desk top and the frame, intending to force the lock. But he hesitated at the damage it would cause.

"You want to get into that?" Edith said from the door.

Stephen nodded.

"Push the pins out of the hinges."

"Hinges?"

"On the back," she said with studied patience as if he was being a particularly stupid child.

"Hinges, back. Right." Stephen turned the desk to get at the hinges. Sure enough, there was a pair of bronze ones holding the slanted board to the desk's back. He inspected the pins, which were just little rods of bronze. They seemed to be in there pretty firmly. They wouldn't come out without the help of a tool, and of course he had brought nothing sufficient for the task.

He'd have to improvise.

All he had handy was his dagger. He drew it and set the point against the top of one of the pins. "Hand me your dagger, Gilbert," he said.

Gilbert put down his book, curious now at what was going on. He handed over his dagger.

Stephen held it by the blade and, using its pommel as a hammer, began to tap the head of his own weapon. The pin resisted for a couple of taps, then began to slide through the hinge. After a few more taps, the width of the dagger point prevented Stephen from forcing it any further. But it had come out enough that he was able to grasp the other end of the rod with his fingers and worm it out the rest of the way.

The other rod came out the same way.

He set aside the top.

As expected the interior of the desk was filled with documents, most of them parchment, but some of them written on Italian paper and vellum. They were covered with writing, mostly in English, some in French. Stephen began laying them out one by one. Two of them consisted simply of lists of names. On one list, there were a series of numbers entered. It looked like an account of payments made in shillings and pence and, on occasion, in pounds. Often there were multiple payments noted in what looked like different inks and pens, although with the same hand. Stephen spotted a familiar name on the list, one Hamo, although whether it belonged to the Ludford vicar was impossible to tell. The other list simply held names. Four of them were marked through with wavy lines.

Looking over his shoulder, Gilbert sighed heavily. He put his finger on the list that looked like an account. "I'll wager those are Baynard's spies and these are his accounts of how much he's paid them."

"Yes," Stephen said. "But what of this other?"

Gilbert stroked his chin. "The barons' men?" He indicated one of the names. "I knew that fellow. He used to come up here on business and stay at the inn. A squire from Hereford. But I had word not long ago that he was killed. A robbery, they said."

"Bromptone said that the kings' men killed a barons' spy in Hereford."

"So this could be Baynard's enemies list."

"So it seems."

"What'll we do? Men would die if those lists became known."

A terrible idea flitted through Stephen's head: he could sell one list to one faction and the other list to the other, and profit doubly from this find. How he could use the money. It was certain to be substantial. But he said, "Nothing."

Stephen continued searching the box.

At the bottom of the pile, he came across a folded scrap of vellum. It was a narrow, ragged, uneven piece, as though it had been cut from a letter. It had been sealed with a daub of green and white wax, a few flakes of which still clung to the leaf. Stephen opened the fragment. A message was written there in a blocky hand: "I need to see you. Across from the Broken Shield After Compline."

He was sure he'd found the note, but it was so cryptic that it gave him no clue who had written it. And alone it would not be enough to exonerate Peter Bromptone.

"He's coming," Edith hissed, her eye pressed to a crack in the door.

Stephen plunged the note under his shirt and scooped up the remaining parchments and papers, which he dumped hurriedly in the box. He put the lid back on. He slid one pin in. There wasn't time to restore the other. He'd have to think of another way to get rid of the servant first.

Footfalls thudded on the floorboards outside. The latch rattled. Stephen snatched a book from the shelves and flung it open. To his astonishment, it was a beautifully illustrated book on sword-and-buckler fencing, showing two men in blue and greenish-brown priestly robes poised against each other, one in the under-arm ward and the other in half-shield. The marginal text explained in Latin what they were doing. He had no more than a moment to admire it before the door swung open.

The boy entered carrying a wooden tray bearing wine cups and a pitcher. Stephen began a smile that froze momentarily on his face.

Behind the boy came Clement, his black shirt and red hose stained from travel, and Muryet.

"You've found the library, I see," Muryet said.

"I had no idea that Baynard was a fencer," Stephen said with more heartiness than he felt. "Look at this! It's astonishing! Marvelous! What a work! Unparalleled in England, I have no doubt!"

Muryet grunted.

"You've an interest in fencing?" Clement said.

"Of course. A most essential manly art. And you?"

Clement nodded shortly.

"Do you think," Stephen asked almost too breathlessly, "do you think the widow might part with this?" He held up the book.

"I doubt you could afford it," Clement said. "It cost as much as a fine horse."

"Oh," Stephen said, putting as much disappointment into the syllable as he could. "Well, perhaps one day. Say, do you think she'll let me consult it now and again?"

"I'm sure," Clement said without conviction. "If she doesn't sell it first."

Stephen returned the book to the shelf. He was sorry he hadn't the time to look at it more, although sword-and-buckler wasn't an art he regularly practiced. It was a civilian's art, and he had been a soldier. "I understand that the earl's men practice every morning at the castle. We'll have to take a turn together sometime."

Clement looked sour. "I doubt they'll let me."

"Oh," Stephen said lightly. "Too bad. We'll have to find another place to meet then." He said to Gilbert, "Are you through? Dally long here and all the food will be gone."

"Quite right," Gilbert said.

They took the wine cups and streamed out of the room under Clement's and Muryet's suspicious eyes.

As the servant closed the door, Stephen saw Clement place his hands on the lid of the desk.

"I think we'd be well advised to leave as quickly as possible," Stephen said.

"Better sense never came out of your mouth," Edith said.

Chapter 19

The hall of the Broken Shield was deserted when the three returned. Dinner was over and the refuse of it had been cleared away. The guests had gone about their business, and only Jennie and Oliver, a manservant, were there sweeping the floor.

Gilbert settled by the fire as Edith inspected the floor under Jennie's anxious eyes.

Stephen fled to the yard in case a dispute over cleanliness arose. He wondered if Harry had returned from the church and was about to go into the stables to check on him when he caught sight of Amicia at a fire burning before the inn's small orchard.

She stood by the fire stirring the contents of a large iron kettle with a long-handled wooden spatula. Her back was to him, and she was unaware of his presence. She had worn her hair piled up on her head, but now it was down, tied at the back of her slender swan's neck with a green ribbon. The delicate profile of her cheek was visible from this angle. He could have stood there for an hour and admired her.

But she turned and broke the spell. She said, "Come to check on your laundry? I shall not abuse it."

Stephen looked into the kettle, where he saw his shirts and hose.

"I'm sure it's safe in your hands," he said, noting as he spoke how red and chapped her fingers had become in only a few days.

He held the note out to her. Their fingers brushed as she took it. He felt light-headed at the touch.

Her brow wrinkled in a question. "What's this?"

He crossed his arms, watching her reaction closely.

When he said nothing, Amicia unfolded the parchment. Her eyes swept over the writing and rose to meet his. "I don't understand," she said, puzzled.

"Do you recognize the handwriting?" Stephen asked.

Amicia shook her head.

"It's not Peter's?"

"No."

"And not yours."

"Of course not."

Stephen took the note back. "Whoever wrote this note killed Baynard. It was sent to lure him out after dark."

Amicia said, "And you thought we wrote it!"

"No. It came from another. But I had to be sure it wasn't you, just the same."

Amicia grasped his forearm. The tingles he'd felt at the brush of her fingers were nothing compared to this. She said, "Tell me! Who is it?"

He was about to say Fitzsimmons, but the name stuck in his throat. Although he had been certain until this instant, a pang of doubt stayed his tongue. Johanna's face loomed in his mind.

Stephen coughed to clear his throat. "I'd rather not say yet. Not till I'm truly sure."

Amicia withdrew her hand. Her brown eyes were large as she held his. "We shall have to trust in you, sir. Please do not fail us."

Chapter 20

Stephen slowly folded the note and slipped it in his pouch. Johanna . . . could it really have been Johanna? Johanna had five pounds coming from Baynard's will, ten if you counted the dowry, which she was sure to control, a fortune for someone in her position. People had been killed for far less money than that. What if she was the one, not Fitzsimmons? It seemed a long shot, but could he afford to ignore the possibility?

"Stephen?" Amicia said. "Are you all right? You look ill."

"I'm fine," he said awkwardly. "Fine." He added abruptly, "I must be going. Got things to do."

"Of course."

He turned away. As he reached the corner of the stable, he heard the splash and swish of the ladle in the cauldron. Amicia began to hum a little tune, Robin in the Thistle. The words for it came to mind. It was a cheery little song celebrating a robin's cunning victory over a hungry weasel. The robin lures a weasel who wants to eat her babies into a thicket where he impales himself on a thorn. It was a popular song, and everyone always laughed in the end at the cleverness of the robin. Stephen wondered if she liked it for the tune or the words. He wished he could be as cunning as the robin, but he felt as though he was stumbling blind from one thing to another. If Peter had not killed Baynard, whoever had done so had planned it out and acted boldly, so that no one would know who had done it. How could he really suppose he might catch such a clever killer?

He suddenly felt like getting drunk, for release from his fears and doubts and regrets at the bottom of a tankard, but instead he went into the stable. The mare was at her oat bag and didn't like having to give it up. She even tried to nip his shoulder when he took it away. He scolded her but it seemed to make no impression, for she then tried to step on his foot. So he gave her back the bag and let her finish the oats while he readied his riding tack and pondered what to do. When she had finished the oats, he put on the saddle and bridle, fingered the sword in its saddle scabbard for no good reason other than the reassurance it was there, mounted, and rode out of the yard.

When he emerged from the shadows of Bell Lane to the openness of Broad Street, the full force of the afternoon sun made him blink. The day had started with a chill, which had lingered through most of the morning, but now the day had grown so hot that Stephen removed his coat and folded it on the saddle pommel. At the foot of Broad Street by the gate there was no sign of Harry, which was odd. Stephen squeezed around a cart blocking the gate, getting a good whiff brine from the barrels it carried.

Outside the town, Lower Broad Street dropped between more timbered houses to the three-arched stone bridge over the river. Stephen felt heavier with every step as he and the mare mounted to the top of the arch of the bridge, the horse's iron shoes clinking loudly on the paving stones in the windless sultry air. It was a day for sitting in the shade with a cool bowl of ale and a plate of sliced apples, not for watching your back for armed men or chasing suspicions.

Beyond the river, the road climbed the hill to the Ludford church, which stood quietly at the top of the rise, surrounded by its cloak of elms. The green of the leaves went well with the whitewash of the church.

From the church, there were two ways to get to Johanna's place, down the road to Richards Castle, skirting the village proper, or through the crooked lanes between the houses. The crooked lanes were the longer, more indirect route, but Stephen just let the mare pick her own way. Villages, even small ones, were always busy places, and Ludford was no exception. There were women active in their gardens, doing or hanging laundry, shouting at children. He passed a wagon full of wheat stalks being brought in from the fields where they had been stacked to dry, and already he could faintly hear the thudding of flails at work in the threshing barn as someone got a head start on the threshing. The ring of a smith's hammer sounded intermittently. He passed a group of children playing hide and seek, and another further on playing football in the street using an inflated pig's bladder for a ball.

It wasn't long before he reached Johanna's tavern. Stephen stepped the mare across the ditch into the yard and dismounted. He heard no voices from the house. No fires seemed to be going in the rear, where they normally would have been brewing ale. Baynard's funeral apparently worked a holiday, though come to think of it, he had not seen either Johanna or Pris at the funeral mass. He was beginning to think that no one was home even before he lifted a hand to pound on the door.

His hand poised in mid-knock as he heard a rustling on the roof. A rustling on the roof by itself wasn't extraordinary. Rats, mice, owls, and other creatures often nested there. But this was louder and more insistent than normal. Stephen looked up to see an arm emerge from the thatch. It withdrew. Two hands enlarged the hole and presently a head and shoulder thrust into view. It was Pris. She saw him and her eyes widened with fear. She said soundlessly, "Please don't tell."

Stephen heard the voices then. They belonged to Johanna and Clement in low but earnest conversation in the tavern's main room to the right so muffled that he couldn't tell what they were saying.

Meantime, Pris had wormed her way out of the hole. She sat on the steep roof, clinging to a cord binding some of the thatch together. From the ground it was only about six feet from the lip of the roof to the ground, and only about eight or nine feet from where Pris had made her hold. But it probably looked farther to her than to him. She was reluctant to let go.

Stephen walked the horse directly beneath her. Grasping the edge of the roof, he stood in the saddle. He held out his hand. She looked at him anxiously but did not move.

"Are you coming or not?" Stephen asked. "The longer you tarry, the more likely they'll catch you."

Pris nodded abruptly and reached inside the hole. She removed a wool satchel and a bundle that looked like a rolled-up dress. Clutching them under her arm, she slid down the roof, catching Stephen's hand. With some difficulty, she managed to plant her feet on the horse's rump. Together, they sank to the mare's back.

Stephen directed the mare eastward toward the river. It was less likely that Johanna and Clement in the tavern room would see them if they went that direction. Pris clasped him about the waist as if she was afraid of falling off.

"Running away, are you?" Stephen said conversationally.

He felt her nod. "They want me to get married."

"That's not such a bad thing, is it?"

Pris snorted. "They want me to marry a grocer."

"Oh? Who?"

"Clement's nephew, Humbert Thame."

"Thame, Thame . . . I've heard of that family. They're well off. It's probably a good choice."

"I don't like him. He picks his nose and smells." She shivered. "The thought of him touching me makes my skin crawl."

"You want to marry Edgar Carter instead."

Pris sat back. "How did you know?"

"I saw you two a few days ago. On the river. Been meeting secretly, have you?"

"Mother found out. She was furious. She beat me with a stick. I still have the marks on my legs. See for yourself." Pris pulled up her skirt. There were old, yellow bruises on her shapely calf and thigh. "She doesn't approve of Edgar."

"Why not?"

"I don't know. She just says he isn't good enough. That I can do better."

"Every mother thinks her daughter can do better."

"What do you know? You don't have any daughters."

"That's true. But I have a mother and sisters."

"I don't know why mother would be so set against him. She used to let Edgar's father poke her."

"Used to?" Stephen turned in the saddle to look at her face.

She did not respond immediately, and wore a suddenly guarded look.

"I said, used to?" Stephen repeated.

Pris nodded. "They stopped a while ago."

"Molly didn't think so."

"Well, it's true," Pris flared. "Mum hadn't been sweet on old Patrick for months. Not since —"

"Not since what?"

Pris' lips pressed together into an obstinate line.

Stephen had an inspiration. "Not since Clement, eh?"

Pris' widened eyes told him he had hit the target. She looked disgusted and nodded. "He gave her better presents."

"Sometimes sweet words aren't enough," Stephen murmured.

"Edgar doesn't give me presents, but I love him just the same," Pris said hotly.

By this time, they had reached the Ludford church, having passed the football game and the amazed stares from the children at the sight of Pris on his horse. It wouldn't be long before some loose tongue carried word back to Johanna that he'd been the instrument of Pris' flight, and it wouldn't take the brain of a sparrow to figure out where she'd gone. "They'll come for you, you know," Stephen said. "Clement's a hard man. He'll make you go home. Edgar won't be able to defend you."

He felt her shiver. Her arms grasped his waist more tightly. "I'm not afraid of Clement," she said stoutly. But there was a tremor in her voice that said just the opposite. "Or of my mother."

Her sudden tight grip on his waist caused her to lose part of her bundle. The rolled-up dress fell to the ground, the skirt fluttering open.

Pris cried out and slipped from the mare. She knelt hastily to gather up the dress.

But she was too late to prevent Stephen from seeing something that caused him to draw a sharp breath. Stephen swung his left leg over the horse's neck and dropped to the ground. Pris clutched the dress to her stomach and the cast of her eye suggested she was about to run. If she did, there was no way he could catch her. But before she could dart off, he got hold of the skirt. He drew the dress from her grasp. There was a dark crusty brown stain on the lower right part of the hem of the white linen. He was well familiar with such stains.

"That's a blood stain," he said.

Pris was breathing hard.

"How'd it get there?"

Pris didn't answer.

"Your mother doesn't want this dress found, does she," Stephen said.

Still, Pris didn't answer.

"This is Patrick Carter's blood, isn't it," Stephen went on implacably.

Pris nodded jerkily. Her fingers worked spasmodically. "She didn't kill him, I swear! She didn't have anything to do with it!"

"But you were going to blackmail her with this dress. It was your insurance, so she wouldn't interfere with you and Edgar, once you were free and away."

"They made her be silent! They said they'd kill her!"

"Who did?"

Pris looked panicked. She didn't answer.

Stephen took her firmly by the arm. "I think you better tell me everything."

Stephen guided Pris through the churchyard to the door of the church, which faced west, like the doors of all churches. The vicar occupied a stool before the door. His face and upper body were bathed in a shaft of golden light that pierced the overhanging elms. A pair of boys about seven or eight were seated cross-legged at his feet. They had wooden tablets covered with a thin layer of wax on their laps and styluses in their hands. The vicar rose in surprise.

"Hello, Uncle Hamo," Pris said.

"Priscilla! What's going on?" He followed them through the door, concern on his face.

"Continue your lesson, vicar," Stephen said. "We've some short business in the church. It's nothing."

"Men," Hamo said sternly, "do not make a habit of dragging young girls into my church and then call it nothing."

It occurred to Stephen that Hamo might think he intended to lie with Pris. Quiet churches, deserted in the middle of the day, were favorite trysting places. "My intentions are honorable," Stephen said. "She just has some questions to answer."

Hamo watched them, his mouth set in a mixture of indignation and indecision. Stephen regretted not interrogating Pris on the street. Hamo seemed set to interfere. He hadn't known he was her uncle. Pris tugged as if she wanted to get free. Stephen worried that if he let go, she'd run.

Then Pris said, "It's all right, Uncle Hamo. He just wants to talk to me."

Hamo grunted, unconvinced. "I'll be within earshot," he said. "Let not the least untoward thing happen." He went out, shooing the two boys in front of him, who had peeked around the doorway.

Stephen relaxed but did not release his grip. Then he led Pris through the nave to the altar, which lay in a rounded apse at the east end of the narrow building. He put her hand on the altar and pressed it down with his own.

"Before God and all the saints," he said as sternly as he could manage, "swear that what you're about to say is the truth."

Pris looked frightened. She hadn't anticipated having to give such an awesome oath. She hesitated, her eyes wide, but she found the courage to bargain. "If I swear, will you make sure I get to Edgar? You won't take me home or to gaol?"

Stephen worried that he'd have to get her talking fast before Hamo went to Johanna's for help. "I'll take you to Edgar's."

"Swear it yourself, then."

"I swear before God and all the saints that if you tell me the truth, I'll take you to Edgar."

Pris relaxed slightly. "Then I so swear as well, before God and all the saints that I will not lie."

Out of the corner of his eye, Stephen saw Hamo stick his head around the door frame to see what they were doing. Hamo jerked his head back.

Stephen removed his hand. He said, "Then tell me about the stain. How did it get there?"

The rain had persisted for days. It fell in a steady gentle downpour, pattering on the straw roof, whispering against the shutters, dappling the puddles in the yard and road, and filling the ditches. The adults were wet and miserable and grumpy; the children chafed at being kept indoors by their mothers. Not a few, however, somehow managed to escape the confines of their dark cold houses for the outdoors, and when Pris went outside the tavern on this chore or that, she often saw boys and girls racing floats in the ditches or running in the muddy lanes, getting filthy. She wished she could join in the fun, although she was much too old for racing floats or playing tag. She had work to do, and mother was in no mood to let her shirk it, even on a day like this.

Because of the rain, business was slow. No, it was more than slow. It was dead. Yesterday, they had had only three customers all afternoon and evening, and no one had stopped in to stay the night, as often happened, since the tavern was just off the road to Richards Castle and caught travelers who were too late to get into Ludlow before the gates closed.

The weather, the lack of business, and some unwelcome news had kept Johanna in a bad mood. She stalked around the inn, muttering under her breath. Once she had cuffed Pris for a bit of back talk, so Pris was sulking too.

Mother was formidable, but Pris was no longer frightened of her. She was a grown woman now and would do what she wanted. She had made up her mind that she was going to run away with Edgar. They were going to marry. It had been her deepest and greatest secret. She had not shared it with anyone, except her best friend, Gunnora.

But Gunnora hadn't been able to keep her mouth shut, and let the secret slip to her own mother.

Two days ago, Gunnora's mother had told Johanna.

When Edgar had come with his father yesterday, Johanna turned them away. They were no longer allowed to see each other.

As nightfall descended to darken an already dark world, Pris, who was seated at last by the fire, heard the latch rattle in the front door. A man's steps were audible in the hallway outside. Then a figure filled the dim rectangle of the door.

"Hello, Pris," Patrick Carter said. He had that strange lilting accent common to the Irish. He'd been in the country a long time, but for some reason had never lost it. "Your mother at home?"

"She's out back feeding the pigs and goats," Pris said, who was glad to have escaped that dirty chore.

"Ah, well, I'll just have a seat and wait for her, then." He found a place at a bench and table and settled down.

"Cup of ale for you, master carter?"

"Don't mind if I do. Don't mind at all."

"It's sure to warm you up. Nasty evening."

"It surely is."

Pris poured out the ale from a clay jug and set the wooden cup before Patrick. "Where's Edgar?"

"I thought it better if he didn't come."

"Why not?" Pris had been hurt that Patrick had come alone, but at least now she could see there was some explanation for it.

"I've business with your mother. It's better we do it together and not while the pair of you are running off to some dark corner." Patrick grinned.

Pris couldn't help but smile, even though she wondered what was up. Patrick had an infectious grin. He made you want to smile when he smiled and laugh when he laughed. Edgar had his father's talent. It was one reason she loved him so much.

Presently, Johanna was audible in the hallway. A bucket clunked hollowly against the dirt floor. Feet scraped. After a moment, Johanna appeared in the doorway. She moved to the fire and sat on a stool, hugging her knees.

"Nasty night for you to be about, Patrick," she said after a while.

"Can't pass up the best ale this side of the Teme," Patrick said.

"I reckon it isn't the ale you've come for," Johanna said. "It never was."

"It's a good excuse. But if I told you I came just to look at you, you wouldn't believe me."

Johanna smiled wanly. "You never give up, do you."

Patrick pushed out a lip. "You never get what you want if you do."

"It's too late, Paddy."

"For us, maybe, but not for our young ones."

Johanna frowned. "That can't happen."

"Come on, now, Jo. Don't be so set in your mind. I've a proposition to make."

"There's nothing you can offer that will change my mind."

"You could at least do me the courtesy of hearing me out. For old times' sake."

"Those are long gone old times."

"Maybe so, but the memories ought to be worth something, don't you think?"

Johanna sighed. "All right. Pris, I think you better leave."

"Mamma!" Pris protested.

"Go. Now!" Johanna said sharply.

Pris had no choice but to retreat to the hallway between the two halves of the house. She thought she might linger there to hear what was going on, but her mother barked, "Keep going!" So Pris went into the other room, where she and her mother lived. She kept the door cracked in hopes she could hear what was said. But Patrick and Johanna talked too softly, perhaps anticipating her eavesdropping, for their words to be made out. Patrick's soft, musical voice went on long and soothingly. Johanna answered with short, sharp bites that fell into the conversation like the strokes of an axe. The only thing Pris was sure of was, Patrick was making an offer for her hand on Edgar's behalf. Johanna did not seem to find the offer persuasive. Their voices rose and fell, but even when Pris opened the door wide enough to stick her head out, she couldn't tell what they were saying, except for once, when her mother burst out, "It's out of my hands, you thick-headed fool!"

In the midst of the discussion, Pris caught the unexpected sound of horses in the yard. Travelers! This was an excuse to come out, for the door had to be answered and the guests welcomed. She threw open the front door and found, to her astonishment, Ancelin Baynard standing under the eaves, with Clement behind him.

"Master Baynard," she said breathlessly, backing up so he could enter. She ducked her head in the gesture of submissiveness he liked and expected.

"Good evening, girl," Baynard said gruffly. He shucked his cloak into her waiting hands. Clement gave her his cloak, too, which she hung on pegs by the door.

Hearing the heated voices in the tap room, Baynard asked, "Your mother giving someone a talking to?"

"I'm not sure who's giving a talking to to whom, your honor," Pris said.

Baynard looked surprised. "I'd like to see the man who can get the better of your mother." He grinned and jabbed an elbow into Clement's side. Clement scowled.

They didn't get the chance to enter the tap room because at that moment Johanna stalked into the hallway. "Ancelin!" she said, taken aback. "What are you doing here?"

"On our way back from Hereford and got held up on the road. A thrown shoe. Have you anything for supper?"

Johanna did not get the chance to answer. Patrick chose that moment to come out. He was wiping his chin, as though he'd just spilled ale as he polished off the last of his cup.

"You'll not reconsider," he demanded of Johanna.

"No!" she said sharply. "Not now. Not ever."

Patrick took her by the arm. She shook him off.

"Is this man bothering you, Johanna?" Baynard said.

"No, he was just leaving."

"We're not good enough for you, then," Patrick said bitterly.

"It's over, Paddy. Now, go, before it starts to rain harder."

"Not good enough for what?" Baynard said.

The fatal question hung in the air.

Johanna's eyes shifted back and forth, finally fixing on a spot on the floor. "He wants permission for his son to marry Pris."

Baynard looked Patrick up and down as if he was seeing Patrick for the first time, although they knew each other. Ludlow was too small a town for them to be strangers, and Patrick had carried Baynard's goods before.

Baynard said haughtily, "Most certainly not."

Patrick eyed him narrowly. "I don't know what you got to say about it."

"I've got quite a lot to say actually," Baynard said. "She's my daughter."

A fly could have flown into Patrick's open mouth. He looked at Johanna for confirmation. Her down-turned lips were a confession. Patrick said, "A bastard's father who's had nothing to do with his kin ought to have nothing to do with this."

Baynard's face got beet red. He wasn't used to being talked back to this way. He thundered, "No daughter of mine will marry the get of an Irish dog!"

Patrick's mouth worked. "That's the way of it, then, is it?" He hawked and spat. The gob hit Baynard's shoe. Patrick said, "I'd piss on it, too, but I don't want to get dirty." He turned and stalked out the back door.

Baynard was in such a rage that he seemed to have lost the power to speak. Choking noises emerged from his throat instead of words. He stood there for a moment, clenching and unclenching his fists. Then he went out the back door, with Johanna not far behind. Clement paused to get himself a cup of ale, and then he too went into the backyard.

The look on Johanna's face was the only thing that kept Pris in the house. But she cracked the door and looked out with one eye. It was nearly dark as pitch there, but she could make out the four, Patrick retreating toward the direction of the latrine, Clement and Baynard standing together five or six steps away, with Johanna just outside the door only a pace from Pris. Baynard was still making choking noises. Clement seemed oddly unaffected by Baynard's anger. Johanna looked at Pris and closed the door. Pris heard more shouting. Then it was quiet. She dared to crack the door again. She saw the glint of something metal, something long and thin, in Baynard's hand. He was facing her mother. Rain fell on their heads; rain fell about them in a prickling shroud; and they just stood there, looking at each other. Pris realized the thing in Baynard's hand was a dagger. He bent over and gathered folds of Johanna's skirt and wiped the dagger on the linen fabric. Then he put the dagger into the sheath at the small of his back.

Pris had the feeling that something terrible had just happened. She wasn't sure what it was, but it had to be awful, horrible beyond words and measure. She shut the door and fled to her bed in the loft.

Chapter 21

"You knew he was your father," Stephen said.

Pris nodded. "Since I was a little girl. Momma made no secret of it, not that it meant anything. He never showed any interest in me, not even after his only son died last year of the pox. It was always 'Master Baynard' this and 'Master Baynard' that and bowing and curtseying in the few times he ever came around, as if I was a servant rather than a daughter."

"You know, Baynard mentioned you in his will."

"What did he do, leave me a spoon?"

"No, he left you a dowry."

Pris's hands flew to her mouth. "How much?" she asked cautiously.

"Five pounds."

"I can't believe that." She turned away so he couldn't see her face.

Stephen wondered if there was anything more she might tell him. But before he had a chance to think of a question, a commotion at the church door interrupted his thoughts. Voices were raised. Hamo appeared in the door. A stocky figure shoved him violently out of the way and entered, followed by three other men.

Pris whirled about, her eyes wide with alarm. "Clement!"

Stephen thought fast. There was a small cupboard space at the rear of the altar. He stuffed Johanna's blood-stained dress into the cupboard behind a large wooden chalice. "Can you climb out one of those windows?" he asked Pris. The windows in the apse were no lower than the height of his chin. She'd have to jump and pull herself up. But she nodded. "I'll keep them busy. You tuck out the window and run to Edgar's." He owed her that much for the help she'd given him. Now he knew who had killed Patrick. It was a great load off his conscience.

"Thanks!"

Stephen advanced toward Clement, who wore a ferocious smile as he tapped a club against his left palm, and three companions. Like Clement they carried stout clubs.

But it was not Clement who launched the first blow. Clement snarled at one of the others "Get him!" and hung back while the others attacked. As they advanced, Clement edged to the side. It looked as though Clement was planning to come at Stephen from the flank while he was engaged with the man in front.

The only way to get out of this alive was to do the unexpected — immediately.

Stephen lunged forward and punched the first attacker in the face before he had time to launch his blow. The punch caught him full in the nose. His head snapped back and he collapsed, clutching his face, as Stephen twisted the club from his hand. Stephen swung backhanded at the man beside him, clouting him under the ear and he dropped like an ox.

Clement and the last man, having seen the fate of their friends, hung back, watching Stephen warily.

Stephen fell into the fool's ward, stick pointed toward the ground in front of him, and waited for an opening. He wasn't so afraid of two as four, though he could not attack one without exposing himself to the other.

But Clement didn't attack. He glanced past Stephen, to the apse, where he must have seen Pris worm through one of the windows. Then Clement ran out the front door, leaving Stephen and the companion to gape at each other.

Stephen had to stop Clement. He pointed the stick at the other man's face and advanced, snarling, "Get out of the way."

The man raised his hands and stepped back.

"Thank you so much," Stephen said.

He went out the door. Hamo and the two pupils stared at him, open mouthed.

Stephen said, "Where did he go?"

Hamo pointed to the right, toward the bridge to Ludlow.

Stephen's horse wasn't where he'd left her. He looked around frantically and spotted her at the other end of the church graveyard, where she grazed among the headstones. He vaulted into the saddle and gave her his heels. She took off like an arrow, leaping the stone fence that demarked the churchyard with an easy bound, Stephen clutching the saddle pommel in fear he would fall off, for he hadn't taken a jump since he'd lost his foot. The mare seemed to know where he wanted her to go, for he needed hardly more than a twitch of the rein and poke of the heel to change her lead and wheel her right, and then they were pounding down the hill toward the bridge.

For a big man, Clement was awfully fast. Pris had just reached the bridge, and though she was running hard, hair and skirts streaming, he was closing the distance. Stephen wasn't sure he could reach the girl before Clement did. He leaned over the horse's neck and urged her on.

Clement and Pris mounted the bridge to its peak. Clement was nearly close enough to touch her as the mare reached the bottom and pounded up after them. Clement heard them, glanced behind, and put on an extra, desperate burst of speed.

Stephen drew the sword from its saddle scabbard and pointed it at the center of Clement's back, fumbling for the right stirrup with his toe so that when they collided he was less likely to fall off from the impact.

Clement looked back again. He saw the point coming at him, eyes wide in disbelief as he apprehended that death was so near, then threw himself flat to avoid it. Stephen swept by and gathered Pris up with his sword arm. She screamed, but clutched him when she realized who it was.

"That was close," Stephen said.

"God have mercy!" Pris cried.

The mare slowed to a walk at the bottom of the bridge. Stephen looked back at Clement, who was leaning against the bridge wall at the peak, gasping for breath. Stephen turned the mare toward Broad Gate, ignoring the astonished look of the friar in an upper window of St. John's Hospital.

Switching the sword to his bridle hand, he swung Pris behind the saddle. Her arms tightened around his waist and her cheek pressed against his back. For a moment, he remembered other times like this with another woman. Before sadness could envelop him, he thrust the memories from his mind.

"Edgar's is that way," she said, pointing to the right.

"I know. But I don't think you'll be safe there. At least, not until you're married. I'm taking you to the Broken Shield. Clement can't get you there, I don't think. We'll send word to Edgar and he can come see you."

Stephen felt her nod.

The warden at Broad Gate stood in the center of the gateway, barring the way with his bill, which normally spent its time leaning against a wall. He'd seen the chase, and his duty to keep the peace had roused him from his usual lethargy. But he shrank back to let Stephen pass as Stephen hadn't scabbarded the sword, and the warden lacked the inclination to test Stephen's temper. Stephen thought, the whole town will know about this before sundown.

Harry was back at his place by the gate. "Good lord," Harry said, "what was that about?"

"Nothing," Stephen said.

"Nothing my ass. You steal her for the dowry? Didn't think you were that hard up."

"Another lucky man has the dowry coming, not me."

"You stole her for somebody else?" Harry asked, incredulous.

"No, she stole herself. I'm just giving her a ride."

With a wave, Stephen squeezed the mare with his heels. She began to trot up Broad Street.

Chapter 22

The Broken Shield was settling down to supper as Stephen escorted Pris downstairs, having temporarily settled her in a room. The serving girls were setting the places, the guests were drifting in, and craftsmen and families who either did not have kitchens or who had no inclination to cook trailed through the front door to mingle in buzzing groups before platters of food were brought in from the kitchen. Supper was a lighter meal than dinner, but it could be substantial nonetheless, for late-arriving travelers often were hungry. Tonight there was an unidentified fish soup, salted red herring in a mustard and lemon sauce, boiled leeks, and bread. Nobody much cared for salted herring, but as a public house, the Broken Shield could not afford to ignore the fast as many families did in the privacy of their homes and have meat, for as a Wednesday this was a fish day. Ludlow was far from the sea and often all that could be had on fish days was salted herring.

Pris did not seem to mind the herring, and she dug into her bowl with relish.

Amicia came in and settled on the bench across the table. She regarded Pris with curiosity. She was about to speak when Pris gasped and grabbed Stephen's arm. Stephen followed her gaze to the doorway. Clement stood there, surveying the room. He caught sight of them. Stephen worried he would come in and prepared himself for a confrontation. But then Clement backed out and disappeared.

"He'll get me here too," Pris wailed.

"Get you here?" Amicia asked. "For what?"

"I've run away to get married," Pris said. "He wants to force me back."

Amicia's eyes narrowed coldly and fixed on Stephen. "I had no idea . . ."

"Not to me," Stephen said.

"He just helped me get away," Pris cut in. She told the story of her flight in elaborate detail. She spoke at such length that Stephen worried that she'd say things about Baynard's death that were better left unsaid at the moment. But perhaps her plan for future blackmail stayed her tongue on that subject, because she left out the part about Baynard and the interlude in the church. She added, "Stephen says I have a dowry coming, so I can afford to marry whomever I like."

Amicia was suddenly angry. She threw down her napkin and stood up. "Spent your day rescuing tavern girls, did you? There isn't much time left, you know. The justice will be in town tomorrow!" She stormed up stairs, nearly in tears.

"What was that about?" Pris asked, taking another helping of herring. "Did I say something wrong?"

"No." Stephen said. "More ale? That fish makes you thirsty."

"It does that," Pris said, holding up her cup. "Not a bad sauce, though. I wonder how they make it."

"Edith won't reveal her secrets, I'm afraid, even under torture." Stephen waved at Jennie, who had the ale pitcher. She came over and poured for them. Stephen said, "What's this about the justice being here tomorrow? I thought he wasn't supposed to arrive until next week."

"A couple of his clerks came in earlier this afternoon," Jennie said, wiping up a little spill on the table. "Booked rooms for those who won't be staying at the castle. Said the main party would be arriving tonight. Court's to be Thursday now. A messenger came by earlier with a summons for you. He said he'd be back."

As Jennie turned away, Pris chattered lightly, "What's so important about that to have you frowning so?"

"That woman's husband —" Stephen pointed a thumb at the stairs "— will be tried for murder then."

"Oh. Who'd he kill?"

"Baynard."

Pris's mouth fell open. "He k-k-killed Master . . . my father?"

"That's what they say."

"Huh," Pris grunted. Her mouth was hard and her eyes narrow. "Why was she upset with you?"

"I was the coroner on the jury that indicted him," Stephen dissembled. "I'll have to testify at the trial."

"Oh," she said and went back to her herring and mustard. Then she said with unexpected insight, "But you have doubts. Even though there was a witness."

"The witness didn't actually see the killing."

"That's true. But there can't be much doubt, can there?"

"No, not much," Stephen conceded.

"Well, then." Pris lost interest in this line of conversation. She broke off a piece of bread to sop up the remaining mustard sauce in her bowl, and began to chatter about how Edgar planned to buy another wagon, a big one this time, and start a regular run between Ludlow and London. "There's not much regular carriage business between them," she said. "He's sure to make plenty of money!"

"I hope so," Stephen said.

"We'll use the dowry to buy the wagon and a team of horses." Her eyes were full of dreams as she went on about a house, furniture, children, clothes, food.

Stephen let her prattle on — dreams, after all, were often the only thing that sustained people — too appalled by the news of the justice's arrival to contemplate anything beyond the prospect of failure. He had no time now, no time at all.

As supper concluded, most of the diners began to rise, and as the servants cleared the tables, a big, black-bearded man clad in a black coat and black hose — all about him was black except the white metal of his sword and dagger and the silver buttons on his coat — came in. The man spoke to Jennie at the door. She pointed Stephen out to him. The newcomer crossed the room, left hand resting on the pommel of his sword. Stephen watched him approach. He put a hand near his dagger and the other on the edge of the table to tip it toward the new arrival if he made trouble.

The black-bearded man stopped by the place where Amicia had sat directly across from Stephen. "You're Stephen Attebrook?"

"At your service."

"My name is Gervase Haddon. I am a knight in service to Nigel Fitzsimmons. I am directed and required to say that he accepts your challenge and will meet you at the appointed time and place on Friday."

"Please tell Sir Nigel that his answer is welcome. I'll see him then."

"I will most gladly, sir." Haddon bowed and backed away a few steps, then wheeled as smartly as if he was at court, and marched out of the hall.

"What was that about?" Pris asked.

"A little nothing," Stephen murmured. He couldn't relax until Haddon had disappeared. He breathed deeply. "Well, we shall have to find a way to get word to Edgar that you're safe now, won't we?"

Chapter 23

The great hall of Ludlow castle had already filled almost to capacity when the prisoners were led in, chained at the neck. A pair of sheriff's bailiffs in the lead, carrying staves, cut through the crowd like the prow of a ship, while the undersheriff bringing up the rear shouted for everyone, since people had begun to hoot abuse at the accused as if they had already been condemned and were on their way to their reward, to be silent or face ejection.

As the prisoners neared Amicia, she, unlike others in the mass, did not give way until pressed aside by one of the bailiffs, and then she remained close enough to reach out for Peter's hand.

But a bailiff struck Peter on the wrist as he groped for her. He cried out and before he could make another attempt, they had moved beyond the crowd to the prisoners' bar, which stood at an angle to the justice's table. The bailiffs herded the prisoners behind the bar and took positions around them, as if there was some danger they either would bolt or lunge for the justice.

Peter fingered his neck ring to relieve its chafing and his eyes wandered the crowd as he sought out Amicia, who had become lost in the press. His eyes paused on Stephen and their gazes locked, but Peter's eyes fell away, all sign of hope crushed at Stephen's stern expression, although it was meant to cover embarrassment and not condemnation or abandonment.

Presently, the jurors filed in and took their seats around the table. There were only ten, though there should have been twelve. Stephen recognized most as knights and major landowners from the northern part of Herefordshire. There were also two burgesses from the town, Leofwine Wattepas, and the head of the goldsmith's guild. A stooped clerk, who looked like he would barely make it to the table without collapsing, shuffled behind them with a writing box and a scroll of parchment. He sank onto a seat, wheezing with the exertion, and unloaded the contents of the box: several goose quills, a pen knife for sharpening the points, and a clay bottle of ink, which he laboriously set out before him with mathematical precision. When he was done, he called sharply for silence in an unexpectedly loud voice.

There was a long pause, as if for dramatic effect. Then two loud knocks sounded on the door by the fireplace. A bailiff entered and stepped to one side. The justice of the eyre strode through the door. Stephen understood the dramatic pause then, because he recognized the justice.

The clerk clapped his hands twice. The men around the table rose to their feet with a scraping of chairs. The clerk intoned in French, "Listen, listen! The court of the King's Bench is now in session, the honorable Ademar de Valence presiding."

De Valence took his own seat beside the old clerk, and all the rest around the table settled with him. De Valance surveyed the room. He was an extraordinarily tall man who seemed to tower over people even when he sat down. His head, which hadn't any hair to speak of now even though he couldn't be much beyond forty, balanced on a stick of a neck. De Valance hid his equally skinny body in a voluminous and rich maroon robe that was trimmed with ermine. He was often seen absently massaging the trim as if to draw attention to the expensiveness of the garment. A massive gold chain that could have done service as an anchor line hung about his shoulders. His hands, a pair of crow's claws, which now lay folded on one another, were well endowed with a stunning collection of jeweled rings. He was from a rich and powerful family and a cousin to King Henry, and everything about him seemed calculated to remind people of those facts.

His black eyes had a hungry look as he ran them over the four men at the bar. Then they strayed to the assembly. They lingered on the lawyer James de Kerseye, drawing a little nod from that great head, which made de Kerseye blush slightly at the acknowledgment. The eyes halted for a moment on Stephen. Valence frowned.

He said in court French, "Attebrook? You here? I thought you were out of the country, soldiering or some such thing, the law having proven to be beyond your modest talents. But evidently soldiering is too, apparently. Now Randall's taken you under his wing. Odd."

"My good fortune, my lord."

"Yes, well, I just hope you don't bollix up your duties as you seem to have done everything else you've tried."

"I shall try not to, sir."

"If your past performance is any guide, we cannot have too much hope for the future."

Valence returned to the men standing before the bar. "Two robbers, a thief and a murderer," he said. "A motley crew. Let's have the first case," he barked.

As the clerk called the case of the thief, Gilbert tugged Stephen's sleeve. When Stephen bent down to hear what he had to say, Gilbert whispered, "Perhaps it would be better if I gave the indictment."

Stephen shook his head. "No, I'll do it."

"I've done it before. He's never shown me such venom."

Stephen patted Gilbert's arm. "We all have to face the fire sometime. No sense running away from it now."

"What does he have against you, if I may ask?"

"Years ago, he was my master."

"And you didn't last."

"Unfortunately not. Lawyering just wasn't for me."

"So . . . you broke the contract."

"Yes."

"To go soldiering?"

"Well, actually I wanted to have my own manor, lord it over the peasants, be the gentleman in my local church, that sort of thing." He paused. "Doesn't look like there's any possibility of that now."

"Funny," Gilbert murmured, "I can't see that of you."

While they had been talking, the jury disposed of the case of the thief. It had not taken long because he had been caught red-handed emerging from the hole he'd made in the wall of a house, clutching the stolen goods.

"You shall hang by the neck," Valence pronounced. "I commit you to the custody of the sheriff, who shall carry out the sentence forthwith."

Since this sentence was passed in French, it did not have an immediate effect on the wrong-doer or his family, who were in the audience. But when the clerk translated it for them, the wife howled and sank to her knees, the oldest son ranted, a daughter cried and turned away, and the defendant himself rattled his chains to such a degree that one of the bailiffs had to hit him over the head to quiet him down.

Valence coldly chided the head bailiff in English, "I insist on better order in the court." He raised his voice to the crowd, still in English, "The next person who creates such a disturbance will be flogged and ejected! Is that clear?"

It was very clear and he got immediate silence, alleviated only by the rustling, coughs and sneezes that always attend even the best-behaved crowds.

The cases of the robbers took slightly more time. A pair of brothers, they preyed on travelers on the road to Richards Castle. Victims had come to appeal against them and to testify, and they were quickly condemned too. The brothers accepted their sentence, when it was translated for them, in surly silence.

"Who'd have thought that northern Herefordshire was such a hotbed of crime," Valence said in English so the local people would not miss his contempt for them. "And now to the murderer." He spoke with more relish than he had about the other cases.

"There is an indictment in this case, I believe," Valence said, gazing over the heads of the crowd at the far wall. "Let's hear it."

Stephen sighed and stepped forward. There was a prescribed way of making the indictment. He had been coached by Gilbert on exactly what to say. Deviation from the prescribed form, as in many legal things, was not only frowned upon as unprofessional, but in some cases could result in nullification of the claim. He hoped his nervousness did not show. Valence would pounce on the smallest deviation from the prescribed form, which had to be delivered in court French. He began, "The accused is Peter Bromptone, of Ditton Priors. The circumstances, as found by the jury after inquest, as these." Valence nodded impatiently, as if hearing the indictment was a formality he could do without. Stephen forced himself not to rush, and related the conclusion of the coroner's jury in the formal manner required of him.

When Stephen had finished, Valence nodded curtly in dismissal.

Stephen smarted even from that little snub, sank back into the protection of the audience and whispered to Gilbert, "Did I get it right?"

"You were fine." Gilbert patted his arm.

Valence swung toward Peter. "How do you answer? Guilty or no?" He spoke again in English on the correct assumption that Peter had no French.

Peter looked startled for a moment, as if he had no idea that the charge against him had just been delivered. "Not guilty!" he blurted. "I didn't do it! I swear —"

"Silence!" Valence thundered. "You are called on to plead, not to explain yourself!"

"Sir, with all due respect —"

"Silence him!" Valence ordered the bailiff.

The bailiff clouted Peter on the head with his staff. Peter sank to his knees under the blow, dragging the others down with him. One of the robbers at Peter's side cuffed him as well.

"You will not speak again until I give you leave," Valence said. "Or you shall have another."

Valence then said to the jurors, "Have the gentlemen of the jury made inquiry into the facts of this case?"

The jury foreman, a knight from Richard's Castle, said, "We have."

"And what have you learned?" Valence asked.

There were no surprises in the foreman's testimony. He told the story of the murder as recounted at the coroner's inquest without any significant deviation.

"And how do you know these things?" Valence asked. The question was a formal one, which he was required to ask at trial.

"From the witness of the Mistress Bartelot, who saw these events with her own eyes, and from the shoemaker Alric, who has a shop at the place where Master Baynard died — practically on his doorstep."

Although it was the job of the jury to inquire into the facts, just as it was at the coroner's inquest, witnesses could be called. Stephen saw that Mistress Bartelot was in the audience, as was Alric and his mother. He had hoped they would come. Last night, he had asked them, but he wasn't sure they would appear. What they might add was Peter's only hope now. This was Peter's opportunity to speak up. Gilbert had coached him in the night about what to do when and if the time came. But he lolled semi-conscious from the blow to the head, blood running down his forehead from a nasty cut on the brow. Unless he spoke out, his last chance would be lost.

"The question, your honor," Stephen said, "put the question to the witnesses."

Valence drummed his thin fingers on the table. "You are out of order, Attebrook."

"Sir Stephen, your honor," the jury foreman said. "It is proper to address him as a knight." The knightly class, for all they might be enemies of each other, endeavored to ensure that the non-knightly class treated them correctly. Valence, despite his family relationships and his power, did not enjoy the position of knighthood, a common lack in bureaucrats these days.

"A knight, you say? He's a knight? I hadn't known," Valence drolled with false ignorance. Of course he'd known. "My sincere apologies, Sir Stephen. But it remains, you are out of order — unless you are Bromptone's attorney. But you can't be. You aren't admitted to the bar. And we forget one small procedural point: he has no right to an attorney to speak for him against the crown. As you should well know from your little time with me."

"But he is allowed to speak for himself," Stephen said, "and to question witnesses — who are here among us."

Stephen was correct on this point and the jury knew it. The jurymen gazed expectantly at Valence, waiting for his ruling. Valence knew he was trapped. He asked Peter, "Do you care to question the witnesses?"

Peter was struggling to his feet. The condemned men on each side helped him up, only because doing so relieved the strain on their own necks. Peter seemed dazed. His eyes were glassy and he swayed.

"What?" Peter said.

"Good," Valence said. "I see not." To the jury, he asked, "Have you reached a verdict then?"

Stephen was appalled that Peter's chance had eluded him. Then he thought of one last desperate thing to do. He said, "He is allowed to ask to be judged by the ordeal."

Valence could barely contain his fury, but only those well familiar with Valence could tell he was angry. His voice often dropped low when his temper was high, and it was so low as almost to be inaudible. He said with in a silky, viperous tone, "You are out of order. Do not let me remind you again not to speak up without the court's leave, or I shall find you in contempt." There was a pause, and Valence added in a louder, more brisk voice, "There is no need for the ordeal. The evidence of guilt is clear."

By law and custom, an accused had the right to call for the ordeal to prove his innocence, but that practice was falling out of use. Valence was within his power to dismiss the call if he judged the evidence of guilt to be strong.

Valence again asked the jury, "Have you reached a verdict?"

Heads nodded around the table.

"What say you — guilty or not?"

"Guilty," all the jurymen said in chorus.

Valence relaxed. He smiled. "Then in the name of the king, I adjudge you guilty. You shall be hanged for your crime, with the others." He added brusquely, "The condemned are remitted to the custody of the sheriff, who may carry out the sentence at his soonest convenience."

There was a shriek from behind Stephen. He turned to see Amicia fall to her knees.

Valence rose and the jury rose with him.

"This court is adjourned," Valence said.

With a sweep of his cloak, he sailed out of the hall.

Chapter 24

As Friday morning dawned, Stephen sat on the edge of the bed, gray disquiet upon his mind. The feeling was as much an old friend as the battle frenzy, a nagging shroud of doubt that was full of questions: Will I fight well? Will I run away? Will I die?

He rose and threw open the shutters, breathing deeply, seeking calm. The air smelled of cooking fires. Dew lay on the windowsill and dampened his hands, which shook so that droplets fell from them. He watched the drops make the long fall to the ground. It was always this way before a fight, the doubt and the shaking. Once things got started, he would forget them. But knowing that did nothing to cast them away.

He washed quickly, his thoughts turning to Peter. The boy was to be hanged at midday, right after the conclusion of St. Michael's feast. Stephen wondered what it would be like to have the noose put round his neck and his feet to dangle in space and to slowly choke and swing. He had seen more than a few hangings; you couldn't avoid them. But he'd never thought until now what it would be like. Poor Peter.

After he poured the old water out the window, he got dressed. This was no ordinary day, and ordinary clothes would not do. By the door, he searched for and found the leather bag containing his mail. He untied the bag and carried the mail shirt and leggings to the window, where he draped them across the sill. He inspected the thousands of interwoven links carefully for rust. Mail rusted easily and had to be constantly tended, or it would lose its proper white appearance that could dazzle in the sun.

Before the armor came the padding, a thick set of linen under-garments. Stephen started by slipping into padded leggings, which he tied to his belt. After that he slipped on the mail leggings. They were like metal stockings and had mail cover for the foot with a leather sole on the bottom like shoes. Taresa had had the mail foot repaired after his own foot was cut off in the hope he would return to soldiering after he recovered. But without the foot he couldn't stay on a horse well enough in a close fight. Then she had died and the heart went out of him. With her gone, with his foot gone, he'd lost hope in the possibility of possessing anything in the future beyond the charity of better men.

After that, he put on the padded gambeson. This was just like putting on a jacket, for it laced up the front. Then came the harder part, the mail shirt. It slipped over the head like a woman's dress, but laced up the back from a point between the shoulder blades to the collar. A proper knight had a squire to help with this part. In the beginning, Stephen hadn't had a squire. He'd had to arm himself, like most poor men-at-arms. Early on, he had learned the trick to it. He threaded the laces through all the ties so that he had only to reach behind his head and tie the laces at the back of his neck. With some careful squirming, Stephen managed to get the shirt on and laced up the first time.

The surcoat came next. It was soft, almost luxurious linen, white on the inside and solid blue, the family color, on the outside. Over the surcoat he belted on the sword, and made sure the dagger was secure at the small of his back. He hefted the strap of the shield over his shoulder, put his coif and arming cap in his belt, and picked up the second sword which would go in a scabbard on his saddle. Last, he found his helmet. It was a big, solid, flat-topped affair that looked rather like a barrel. When he was a child and such helmets had started to come into use, he had laughed at seeing all the knights wearing barrels on their heads. Now he had one. Once it had been painted blue, but the paint had largely worn off. It was a good helmet, but looked a bit forlorn and cheap, all dented and missing its paint. He tucked the helmet under his arm and turned toward the door.

Stephen's appearance, as he jingled down the stairs into the hall, caused some consternation among the guests, who were assembled for breakfast. It was unusual to see an armored man. Even knights and men-at-arms rarely armored up to go about town or the countryside, because it was so uncomfortable and threatening a thing to do. At most they might carry their weapons about, although that normally was frowned upon if not forbidden outright in some towns.

Jennie and Edith met him at the bottom of the stairs. Edith wore a disapproving face; Jennie looked worried.

Gilbert came in through the door to the yard. He was wearing a sword. The wide sword belt looked odd wrapped around his rather large girth and made him appear broader than he was. Stephen hadn't known Gilbert even owned a sword.

"You be careful," Edith said.

"I'm never careful," Stephen said with a smile. "Haven't you understood that yet?"

"Are you sure we shouldn't come?" Jennie asked anxiously.

"No. No need for a crowd. It's a private affair."

He said goodbye and went out the door into the yard. Gilbert followed.

In the stable, he was surprised to see that Gilbert had already saddled the stallion. He checked the girth, tightened it a notch, and mounted. The stallion stamped about, as if ready to run. Gilbert climbed on the mare instead of his customary mule and, carrying Stephen's lance, they rode toward the gate.

"You're old for a squire," Stephen said.

"If any of them laughs at me, I'll split his head," Gilbert said.

Stephen laughed. "The only thing that's missing is my box." Often the participants at formal duels brought coffins made for them, just in case.

"There wasn't time," Gilbert said. "I've commissioned a hole dug 'specially for you in the Ludford churchyard, however. It should be ready by the time we arrive."

"You're too kind."

"Your servant."

Bell Lane was well awake, off to the start of a perfectly normal day. The old woman, Jermina, emerged from the cobbler's shop to sweep off the stoop. Alric's apprentice followed her and began to fold down the window shutters to make counters, signifying the shop was open for business. They exchanged nods and good-days. Inside, Alric laid out a sheet of leather on the cutting table and set a pattern upon it in preparation for cutting a shoe. Mistress Bartelot's upper window was open, as it usually was in the mornings so she could take the sun, but she was nowhere in evidence, although a cup of steaming cider sat on the sill as if she had just put it down.

Broad Street was already filled with people hurrying up the hill toward High. They passed a pretty girl carrying a basket with a cover over its contents who was followed closely by a pair of grim-faced friars in dirty black robes and bare feet. The girl swung her head to watch Stephen, but the friars acted as if he did not exist. Two boys who had been playing ball gaped at Stephen in his armor and ran alongside the horse almost as far as Broad Gate. He ignored them, although he worried how the stallion, always excitable, would react to this.

Fortunately, the gate was clear when they neared it. The warden on duty gave them the once over, top to bottom, but remained speechless on his stool, open mouth revealing his toothless gums.

A few feet away, Harry also gaped at the sight. "Where you going?" he asked.

"Gilbert needs a lesson in manners. He's been so rude lately."

"I can't believe that — not fat old Gill."

Gilbert swung the lance around and leveled its point at Harry. "I'm in a rotten mood, so you watch it."

Harry threw up his hands. "Careful with that thing. You might hurt yourself."

"The pointy end is toward you, my friend. You watch out."

Harry did not reply and they crossed through Broad Gate and trotted down the street toward the bridge.

When they were some distance away, Harry yelled, "Careful you don't fall off that horse, you old fart!"

Gilbert didn't turn around, but he made an obscene gesture in the air.

"You wouldn't believe that he was once a man of God," Harry said to the warden. "What's the world coming to?"

"Don't know," the warden said slowly. "Been going to hell since I was a boy." He swatted at a fly.

Otherwise, it was a quiet normal morning on Broad Street.

"It seems he's changed his mind," Gilbert said.

"So it seems," Stephen said, scuffing the dirt of the path with his good foot.

They were standing in the shade at the churchyard of the Ludford parish church. It was nearly dinner time. They had been waiting four hours and Nigel Fitzsimmons had yet to appear.

"Do you think we should go?" Gilbert asked.

"No, we'll give him more time. Perhaps he got lost."

"Lost his nerve, more likely," Gilbert muttered.

"I've a feeling he's got more than enough nerve."

A babble of voices became audible from the direction of the bridge. A fairly large group of people must be approaching, but it couldn't be Fitzsimmons.

And it wasn't. It was Edgar and Pris at the head of a party of two dozen people. At the sight of them, Hamo shooed off his pupils and came across the yard, waving greetings. He had obviously been expecting them.

"Looks like a wedding, I'd say," Gilbert said.

"A bit rushed, though, don't you think?" Stephen said.

"You're surprised?"

"No, I wouldn't waste any time, if I were them."

Gilbert nodded in the other direction. "Looks like mother has found out. Here she comes."

Johanna and Clement emerged from a lane across the wide street that ran along the south side of the churchyard. They hesitated at the sight of the large party accompanying the bridal couple, which allowed Edgar, Pris, and their friends to enter the gate first. The bridal party trooped through the yard, Molly hanging on Hamo's arm looking triumphant. They stopped at the church door, the usual place for weddings. Johanna and Clement passed the gate and followed, the pair throwing nasty looks in Stephen's direction.

"I believe she'd cut your heart out, given the chance," Gilbert said.

"I have another engagement, and I think that's him at last." Stephen turned to the west. A body of horsemen was approaching at an easy trot on the road from Richards Castle. Fitzsimmons was at the head, mailed, armed, and followed by six knightly retainers. They halted by the gate.

Stephen went out to speak to Fitzsimmons, who scowled. "Odd place for a duel," Fitzsimmons said, crossed forearms resting on the pommel of his saddle. "We can't have something more . . . private?"

"I like it here," Stephen said. He kept his voice nonchalant.

Fitzsimmons grunted in reply.

"How would you like your satisfaction?" Stephen asked, although he already knew the answer.

"To the death," Fitzsimmons spat.

"It's your misfortune. We can start in the street here." Stephen pointed to the place. "I have only one lance, so if you'd be so kind as to limit yourself likewise."

"Of course," Fitzsimmons said with cold courtesy. "I prefer the sword in any case."

"Good, then. It's late. I can't see any reason to delay any longer. Let's get started. No need to appoint a referee, I think. Do you?"

"The sooner this is over the better." Fitzsimmons wheeled his horse and trotted about thirty yards off. There he changed to his warhorse and put on his helmet.

Stephen put on his own helmet, slipped his hands into the mail mittens on the ends of his armored sleeves, and mounted the stallion. Gilbert handed him the lance, and Stephen walked down the street to his own starting place about a hundred yards from Fitzsimmons.

Without a referee there was no one to tell them when to start. So for a long moment they sat there looking at each other.

Stephen began to feel lightheaded. He pressed a heel against the horse's side behind the girth, asking for an immediate canter in the right lead. The horse burst forward, eager to run. Fitzsimmons came forward as well. Before they had started, they'd seemed far apart; now there seemed to be hardly any space at all between them, and that little bit rapidly diminishing. They had only a moment to take each other's measure, to read intentions from posture, the tilt of the shield, the slightest rise or droop of the lance — to gauge the other's determination or cowardice and to guess how he meant to attack.

Stephen angled to make the first pass on FitzSimmon's left.

But Fitzsimmons veered more sharply to get to Stephen's right, thinking no doubt that without a left stirrup, Stephen could be thrown more easily from the saddle if struck from that direction.

Fitzsimmons rose in the stirrups and leaned forward, lance point steady on Stephen's face like, the perfect marriage of horse and man.

The horses thundered on the hard-packed surface of the street, their hooves throwing up clods of dirt. The members of the wedding party had abandoned the church doorway and lined the fence along the road, their mouths open and moving as if they were shouting. But sound seemed to have gone from the world, which had shrunk, as if to a mere tunnel containing only Fitzsimmons in his black and white tabbard and the sinister spark of sunlight off the tip of his lance.

Stephen let his point sag into the boar's tooth guard, then snapped it up at the last instant, intending to deflect Fitzsimmons' lance while at the same time striking his own blow. But Fitzsimmons must have seen through the trick, because he brought his point down toward Stephen's body and leaned upon the pole with his shield so that Stephen felt like he was striking a tree limb. Fitzsimmons' lance slithered along the length of Stephen's and crashed into his shield, which he swung across the saddle at the last moment to take the hit.

The impact was like a hammer blow to Stephen's arm and drove the shield hard against his chest, and for a moment he thought the arm was broken. He fought to remain in the saddle, gripping hard with his knees. Had it not been for the high cantle, he would have fallen.

Then they were past each other and the horses were wheeling as if on their own, Fitzsimmons casting away the remains of his lance, which had shattered at the impact, and drawing his sword.

Fitzsimmons spurred his horse to close the gap. Stephen shortened his grip on his lance and stabbed underhanded as Fitzsimmons drew up, but his point met only the air, for Fitzsimmons set it adroitly aside with his sword.

And then they were side to side. Stephen tried to hit Fitzsimmons with his shield, but the other man ducked, grasped the top of Stephen's shield and pulled him from the saddle. Lacking a stirrup on the left side, Stephen had nothing to prevent his fall, and he crashed to the ground.

Stephen rose to his knees with difficulty. He gasped for breath. His helmet had come off. He groped for it, caught it and looked up to see Fitzsimmons leaning over, his sword held high and about to descend on Stephen's head. Stephen threw himself to the right, rolled between the legs of his own horse and stood up, keeping his animal between himself and Fitzsimmons. He tried to put his helmet on. His left hand barely obeyed him. His right shook so much that he banged his teeth hard on the helmet's rim.

Sound had returned to the commons, but only as a sigh of wind among the tops of the elms and the flutter of wings as a crow flew across the road. There was no shouting. Open mouths and shocked expressions showed among the would-be celebrants along the fence. Fitzsimmons' men watched grimly, professional squints in every eye.

Fitzsimmons impatiently whacked Stephen's warhorse on the flank with the flat of his sword to get him out of the way. The horse charged to the end of the commons where Gilbert ran to retrieve him. For a moment, the two men regarded each other, panting hard.

Stephen hefted his shield with his numb hand, the feeling slowly returning to it. He tried to draw his sword, but for some reason it would not come out smoothly. After he tugged and tugged, the scabbard finally released it. To his horror, he saw that it had bent sharply in the fall.

Then Fitzsimmons was on him, dealing powerful blows with the sword. They slammed against Stephen's upraised shield, and more than a few thudded against his helmet with stunning force.

Stephen ducked, weaved, and danced, but nothing took him safely out of range of those awful blows. The horse and the man moved as though they were one being. They matched his every step. He could not escape.

Before long, he was so battered that he felt he could not resist the end. He sensed it coming, as if the herald of death had grasped his shoulder. The relentless blows at last caused his shield to split, and it was now only a few boards held together by splinters. He stripped the blasted remnants from his arm as he backed away.

And tripped over the broken shaft of Fitzsimmons' lance.

Fitzsimmons took immediate advantage of his fall and spurred the warhorse to trample him as he lay on the ground.

Stephen grasped the broken pole and rolled desperately away from those enormous hooves.

As he rolled, he came to his knees and swung the pole like a bat against the horse's forelegs.

The Wayward Apprentice

The horse screamed and backed away.

Stephen stood up. His breath came hard and fast, creating droplets of moisture on the inside of his helmet that dripped down the front of his surcoat. He was about at the end of his rope.

Fitzsimmons could see victory in the exhausted droop of Stephen's shoulders. He spurred the horse forward and raised his sword, confident that this blow would bring the end.

Stephen waited for him, the pole held low and behind, a picture of defeat . . . waiting . . . stumbling a little . . . oddly the stumble brought him around to Fitzsimmons' right, a gift to his adversary for there the death blow would be strongest . . . waiting . . .

. . . for the moment when the blow fell.

Fitzsimmons' sword, that shiny ribbon of steel, which glittered in the morning sun like liquid lightning, rose to a great height and then swept downward with a swift song toward Stephen's shoulder.

Now was the time — now!

Stephen met Fitzsimmons' blow with one of his own aimed at Fitzsimmons' hand, as he slipped to the side and under the sword.

There was a sharp crack as the spear pole collided with Fitzsimmons' wrist. The bright sword spun through the air. Admirably, Fitzsimmons did not cry out as he cradled his arm to his chest. Stephen ran for the sword.

He turned and tapped the blade against his leg. He could feel the sword's fine temper as the blade shivered.

"I say, Nigel," Stephen said with far more nonchalance than he felt, "you've lost your sword. Would you like to continue?"

"Allow me another and I'll be glad to go on."

"You're sure? It appears you're hurt."

"I can play as well left handed as right."

"You've fought well. There's no shame in stopping."

"This isn't over yet." Fitzsimmons slipped from his horse and cast away his shield.

"As you wish." Stephen motioned for Gilbert, who came as beckoned, looking puzzled. "I'll need to borrow your sword," Stephen said.

Hesitantly, Gilbert handed the blade over.

Stephen tossed Fitzsimmons' sword back to him. Fitzsimmons caught it with his left hand and stood ready in the plow guard. He held the wounded arm against his chest.

"Thank you, Gilbert. If you will kindly move back and give us some room . . ."

Stephen assumed the left tail guard, the safest of all the guards when caught without a shield, and waited, partly to give himself more time to recover and partly to see what Fitzsimmons would do.

For Stephen had no intention of killing Fitzsimmons. A dead Fitzsimmons was no use to him.

For his part, Fitzsimmons had no such merciful intentions. And he was not so worn out or battered. He launched an attack, lunging with the point. Stephen cut upward in an effort to set it aside. But the thrust was a feint. No sooner than it was launched than it pulled back and became a solid cut to the shoulder, aiming to break bone beneath the mail. Caught unprepared and out of position, Stephen ducked. The blow clanged against his helmet, knocking it askew. He could not see anything but the side of the helmet which should have faced his ear. Stephen sensed that Fitzsimmons was close, very close. A glance at the ground — there were Fitzsimmons feet — told him they would close enough to touch chests!

It was suicide to try to back away — but this close to a man with only one arm! It was a gift! Stephen dropped his sword and grabbed Fitzsimmons around the waist. Just a little lift and the throw would be his, and Fitzsimmons would be defeated!

But Fitzsimmons hooked Stephen's leg and they fell together. Fitzsimmons landed on top and scrambled to mount Stephen's chest. He pried up Stephen's helmet and began to beat him in the face with a fist. The wounded arm was not so wounded after all! It held Stephen's head still while the other fist did the work.

Stephen tried desperately to ward off the blows by sheltering beneath a forearm, but that did no good. Fitzsimmons' fist landed solidly on his neck and chin again and again.

Barely conscious, Stephen realized that by accident his left hand had grasped Fitzsimmons' right wrist. The glimmer of an opportunity presented itself. He roused himself for a final effort. If this did not succeed, there would be no other. Fitzsimmons would win and he would die. As Fitzsimmons raised his left hand for another blow, perhaps the last he would need, Stephen reared up and snaked his right arm over and around Fitzsimmons' right. Straining with everything he had, he managed to reach and grasp his own left wrist. He had achieved the underkey, one of best of the armlocks. He sank back and twisted Fitzsimmons' trapped arm. Fitzsimmons fell forward and to the side, landing hard on his face. Cranking on the lock, Stephen rolled onto Fitzsimmons' back. Then he drew his dagger. He pressed the point to beneath Fitzsimmons' chin.

"Do you yield now?" Stephen panted.

Fitzsimmons hesitated, then nodded.

"The feud," Stephen said, "it's finished?"

Again, Fitzsimmons nodded.

Stephen hauled Fitzsimmons to his feet, but did not release him. "Good. Then we have other unfinished business. In the name of the crown, you'll come with me."

Stephen guided Fitzsimmons through the churchyard gate. The members of the wedding party backed away to clear the path for them, awe and astonishment on their faces.

At the church door, he paused. There was something there that tickled his mind. But he couldn't put his finger on what it was.

Stephen continued into the nave of the church.

Fitzsimmons found his tongue at last. He wheeled on Stephen, who let him go, and demanded, "What's this about?"

"I've some questions to ask," Stephen said.

"I've nothing to say to you."

"You have sanctuary here. I'll not trouble you, no matter what you say. But I will have my answers."

Fitzsimmons' eyes narrowed. "What do you want?"

"Did you fire Baynard's mill?"

Fitzsimmons laughed shortly. "No."

"Did you cause it to be fired?"

Fitzsimmons stood silent.

Stephen pushed him to the back of the nave by the altar. He pressed Fitzsimmons' hand on it, just as he had pressed Pris' hand.

He said, "On your oath and by God, did you cause it to be fired?"

Fitzsimmons looked worried for the first time. At last he said with difficulty, "I gave the order."

Stephen nodded. "Did you have him killed as well?"

Fitzsimmons gritted his teeth. But he said, "No."

"Did you kill him yourself?"

"No, but I wish I had. He deserved it, as much as you do."

Stephen was stunned at the answer. He had been certain that Fitzsimmons was behind Baynard's death. It was the only explanation that made sense. "On your oath?"

Fitzsimmons relaxed and lost the worried look. "On Christ's blood, I had nothing to do with Baynard's death."

Stephen turned away, thinking hard. But if not Fitzsimmons, then who? He had been so sure — so confident that he had wagered Peter Bromptone's life on this single throw of the dice.

He saw the wedding party, which had followed him into the church to see what was up, staring at him in shock and amazement.

He tried to think. He had just seen something important, but his thoughts moved like sludge. His head throbbed like a drum and his right eye could open only a slit. It would be swollen shut before long.

Then the sludge seemed to speak in his mind. Stephen strode rapidly to the church door. Gilbert followed him closely and nearly had to trot on his shorter legs to keep up.

"What is going on, my boy?" Gilbert asked anxiously. "You look like a hound on the scent."

Stephen found the writing tablets by the door and picked them up. Three of the tablets were covered in childish hand. The fourth was in blocky, rather awkward but adult letters, which were familiar.

Stephen's eyes ran over the members of the wedding party. He saw Hamo frowning at him. "This is your hand, isn't it?"

Hamo nodded. "Of course. The pupils copy this work."

"And you are Priscilla's uncle?"

Now Hamo looked astonished. "I am not yet, but will be shortly."

Stephen felt again as if the world had suddenly gone quiet. He swung about and found Edgar in the crowd. He said to Hamo, "So it was to Edgar you gave the note?"

"What note?"

"You remember the note very well — the one commanding a meeting on Sunday night outside the Broken Shield. The note that led Baynard to his death. You know the note I mean."

Hamo's mouth fell open. "I wrote no such note!"

Stephen advanced on Hamo, menace in his voice and posture. "But you did write a note about a meeting at the Broken Shield, didn't you."

Hamo nodded, quaking. "I wrote a note, but I know nothing about Baynard. I had nothing to do with his death."

But there was a false ring to his denial, and while Stephen pressed Hamo, Edgar had edged toward the church door. When Stephen's eyes fell on him a second time, he ran to the altar and placed his hand upon it.

Stephen pressed on again. "You gave the note to Edgar."

"No!" Hamo cried in anguish. He saw where this was going; they all saw it.

Stephen had another revelation. He said softly, "You gave it to Molly."

Hamo's mouth worked.

"She's your sister, isn't she?"

Hamo nodded.

"She asked you for the note."

Hamo nodded again.

The vision of a ledger page swam into Stephen's mind. "She knew Baynard would come because you had informed for him in the past."

As Hamo stammered, Molly made a break of her own, but not to the altar. She tried to shoot past Stephen. He caught her arm. She punched him in the face. The blow landed on his right eye. The pain was so great that he let her go. Gilbert made a grab for her but she fended him off with a stiff arm and vanished through the church door.

Stephen straightened up, cupping his wounded eye, which had now closed completely. He saw with detached amazement that there was blood on his hand.

Gilbert waddled in pursuit, but Stephen called him back. "Let her go. We're not finished here."

The wedding party was shouting, although Stephen had not registered the noise. He pushed through the screen of people and stalked to Edgar, who trembled at his approach. Fitzsimmons, who seemed absorbed in these unexpected and strange developments, watched with folded arms.

"It was because of your father, wasn't it, Edgar?" Stephen said.

Edgar nodded, both hands gripping the altar as if Stephen might try to pry him away from it. "He-he-he killed dad!" He seemed to find courage from somewhere, for he added with greater strength. "Mamma said it was the only way we'd get justice — the old way."

Suddenly Stephen felt heavy and tired. The old way, feud. It was a way open to all, not just to aggrieved knights. The elaborate edifice of the law had not succeeded in eradicating private vengeance. By ancient custom, Edgar had acted properly. But modern justice made no allowance any longer for that old way.

Stephen said, "So you hid in the alley and waited for him."

Chin high, Edgar nodded. Although he was frightened, it was clear he was proud of what he had done.

"You were interrupted perhaps by the argument between Bromptone and Baynard?"

"I waited until it was over and the other man, that fellow Bromptone, stepped away."

"And you killed Baynard with his own dagger. An easy tool to reach if his back was turned."

Edgar nodded savagely. "It was only fitting to use the knife that killed my father."

Stephen had what he needed now to set Peter Bromptone free and to return him to his beautiful wife. But there was a final fatal thread, which had only now occurred to him, still not tied up. He had to follow it until the whole business was done.

"I suppose Pris told you," Stephen said almost off-handedly.

"She told me everything!"

"She didn't see it done, you know. It was dark and raining. She only saw Baynard with a bloody knife afterwards — rather like the Mistress Bartelot saw Peter."

"What are you saying?"

"That Baynard didn't kill your father."

"How's that possible! Pris was there. Tell him, Pris!"

Pris started to speak, but Stephen stopped her with a raised hand. "No, I don't think it was Baynard. He was left handed, and the man who stabbed Patrick struck with the right hand." He swung around. "But there was a man there who is right handed. That man," Stephen said raising a finger at Clement.

Clement's mouth fell open. He turned and ran out of the church, several men from the wedding party in pursuit.

Stephen left the altar and drew up to Johanna, who oddly had not run. He said, "If you don't want to be appealed for murder as an accomplice, you'd better tell me what happened. You were there. You saw it all."

Johanna struggled with the words. "He made me keep silent. He said he'd kill me and Pris if I ever spoke of it."

"But he isn't here any longer."

"No, him, not Baynard — Clement!"

"I don't think you'll be troubled by him either. But you will be by me."

Haltingly, Johanna's story came out: Edgar's interest in Pris, her opposition, Patrick's attempt to win her over, Baynard's and Clement's unexpected appearance, the argument, much as Pris had recounted it to Stephen. "Ancelin always had an ungovernable temper," she said. "It was why I stopped seeing him. He could be jealous and when he was in a rage, he beat me."

"But we're not concerned about you," Stephen said implacably. "What happened in the yard?"

"He lost his temper, as I was about to tell you. He lost it — but gave his dagger to Clement and told him to deal with Patrick." A tear rolled down her cheek. "Deal with him, he said. And Clement — he took the knife and caught up with Paddy at the edge of the field — and drove the knife into his ribs and just walked away. Paddy stood there looking surprised, the rain running off his face. Then he just staggered off across the field, and that's the last I saw him alive." She shook her head. "You know, I loved all three men once. Now two are dead and you're about to take the last one."

Stephen shook his head. He was right at last, but there was thin satisfaction in it. The truth had a habit of turning out to be other than as expected.

The men who'd taken after Clement appeared in the church door. Clement sagged between them. His face was bloody and bruised. Stephen guessed he was lucky to be alive, for these men must have been Patrick's friends, if not relatives. They pitched Clement to the dirt floor and wiped their hands with satisfaction.

Edgar launched himself at the prostrate form with a snarl, but Stephen caught him by the collar and shoved him back toward the altar. "You best stay by the altar if you hope to maintain your claim of sanctuary." He added to the men who'd made the catch, "Find something to tie him with. He'll have to answer to the sheriff."

He turned to the man and the boy by the altar. "As for you two, you've a choice. You can surrender to the crown or you can abjure the realm. I have no power to ignore the crimes you've confessed to, even if I wanted to. Which will it be?"

Fitzsimmons chuckled humorlessly. "I'll abjure."

"And you, boy?" Stephen said to Edgar, who looked anxiously at Pris as she came to his side.

"I've no choice but to leave, haven't I?" Edgar said miserably.

"None, really, if you want to live."

"I'll go then."

Pris wailed and her head sank to his chest.

"She can't go with you," Stephen said. "You have to go alone. You've two days to leave for Bristol. That'll be your departure point."

Pris began to cry harder, and Edgar didn't look far from tears himself. Fitzsimmons seemed unmoved by the pronouncement. He leaned against a wall and spat. He beckoned to Gervase Haddon, and they conversed in terse whispers.

Stephen asked Hamo to fetch the hundred bailiff, and waited for him outside in the shade of the yard. Now that the excitement was over, he was aware how every pore of his body ached. He yearned for a drink and to lie down.

Gilbert hissed in his ear, "It's getting late! We must hurry!"

It was late. By now, most people would be getting up from St. Michael's feast, and Peter Bromptone would soon be hanged. Stephen said, "I have to wait for the bailiff, you're the one who taught me that. You go, tell the sheriff's man we have evidence that will exonerate Bromptone."

"He won't stay the execution without a writ!"

"Then make one. On my authority."

Gilbert blinked dubiously.

Stephen said, "Who'll countermand it? Valence? He's miles away at that manor of his, probably in the midst of celebrating St. Michael's feast as we stand here."

"I was rather thinking the sheriff's man might just ignore it."

"Throw your weight around, invoke Sir Geoffrey's name. Do whatever you have to do. Don't we represent the crown?"

Gilbert stroked his chin. "I suppose we do, at that, don't we? I've never done this, stay an execution. Are you sure a simple writ's the proper procedure?"

"I have no idea, but it has to be."

"What would be the proper form for such a writ?"

Stephen wanted to stamp his foot in frustration. "Just write something, anything!"

"I'll do my best," Gilbert said, and hurried away.

Stephen paced nervously through an agonizing wait until the hundred bailiff rushed up, followed by two of his reeves.

"We've a pair of criminals, a murderer and an arsonist, who've sought sanctuary in the church," Stephen told him. "They've agreed to abjure the realm, so we'll need a watch put upon the church until they've been given the proper clothes and set out. A single man should do it. Round the clock, though, understand? The church shall not be unwatched until they go."

"Right, sir," the bailiff said. "But just one man? That's really not enough. They might try sneaking out one of the back windows, if you know what I mean."

"One should be enough," Stephen said. "Unless you've a few eager men who'd like to volunteer for the work."

"Oh, no. It's hard enough getting men to stand on watch. One man it is, if that's what's wanted. On your authority, sir."

"Good." Stephen stretched. "I need a drink."

The bailiff tugged his hat. "If I may say so, sir, you certainly look as though you need one. You seem to've been through hell."

Stephen smiled. The effort reopened some nasty splits on the inside of his lips. Several of his teeth felt loose, but none had been knocked out. He had been lucky. "Maybe not through hell, but close. Very close."

Wasting no further time, Stephen rushed in search of his horse.

Chapter 25

Stephen careered up Broad Street and turned the corner onto High at the top of the ridge. He swerved around a cart, startling its draft horses. The driver pulled hard on the reins as they reared. He shouted an oath and shook his fist. Stephen ignored him and prodded the stallion with his spurs. It was a straight shot to the castle gate, and there just entering the gate was Gilbert's rotund figure, bumping precariously on the mare. The stallion pounded up High Street, head down, body stretched, long legs reaching for and grasping the ground as he pulled it behind him.

A fair number of people were already making their way up High Street to the castle for the hanging. They heard Stephen coming and jumped out of the way with alarm as he streaked by.

It was less than two hundred yards from the corner of Broad Street and the castle gate, and within moments he had to slow to enter that narrow aperture, although he didn't pause as the watchmen came out of their recesses to see what the commotion was about. They gaped at his battered face and armor, and he could image what they must be thinking: there must have been a calamity, a rising by the barons, an attack by the Welsh, or some such danger; but they made no effort to stop or to question him.

Gilbert was just passing through the inner gate beside the big square tower that had been the fortress' original keep. Stephen cantered across the big outer bailey, passed the scaffold, a long square-cut beam suspended on frames in the shape of the letter A which had been erected beside the path from the outer gate. He was surprised at the size of the crowd already collected there. Large knots of people ranged about the grass. They gaped at Stephen too.

He crossed through that second gate to the much smaller inner bailey. Gilbert was just dismounting before the whitewashed timber hall.

"Oh, hello there," Gilbert said a little breathlessly. "Thought you weren't coming."

"You ride slowly," Stephen said.

Gilbert was miffed. "I had to spare the time to draft your writ."

"You've got it?"

Gilbert produced a roll of parchment from his sleeve.

"I hope it's legible." Stephen snatched the roll and strode into the hall.

"Better than you could do yourself, I've no doubt," Gilbert said behind his back as he followed Stephen in.

The castle's feast of St. Michael had evidently just concluded. The aroma of roast goose hung in the air. Most of the diners had risen from their places and were congregating around the wine barrels along the far wall. Servants had already started taking down the tables and stacking them in the rear behind the fireplace. A pair of greyhounds were snarling over scraps, bumping into people and causing a commotion, some of the squires urging them on. A knight aiming to break up the disturbance grabbed one of the squires by the nape of his collar and flung him toward the main door.

Stephen looked around for Walter Henle, the castle constable and sheriff's senior representative in this part of the county. He spotted Henle still at table.

Stephen made his way through the crowd to the table. The buzz of conversation that had filled the hall dropped off and heads swiveled at his progress. Henle laughed as he drew up, a short sharp bark that sounded unnaturally loud in the sudden silence.

"Good God, man," Henle said. "What happened to you?"

Stephen ignored the question and said, "I'm sorry, my lord, but I've got to spoil your hanging."

"What do you mean?"

"There's been . . . a development."

"A development? What are you talking about?"

"Another man has just confessed to the crime for which Peter Bromptone has been convicted."

"What did you do, beat it out of him?"

"No."

Henle's mouth worked. "This is most unusual. I can't stop his hanging without an order from Justice de Valence."

"I'm afraid you must. I've taken it on my authority as deputy coroner to order a stay of execution." Stephen handed Henle the writ.

Henle unrolled the parchment and read it. He looked up. "I've never heard of such a thing being done. This is out of order."

"The crown can issue stays as well as it can pardons. I represent the crown in this matter."

"You're taking on rather more than your responsibility, young man. De Valence isn't going to like this."

"I'm sure he wouldn't accept the hanging of a man for a crime another has confessed to."

Henle coughed and said slowly with what a cynic might have taken for sarcasm, "Yes, Valence is a man of justice." He slapped the table. "Well, we've three others to dangle today, so the mob won't be disappointed. I don't suppose it matters if we hold back one. We can always hang him later."

"I'd like him released to me."

"No, he'll stay in hold until the justice has had a chance to inquire. The final decision is his."

"Bromptone has a right to bail."

"And I'll not grant it."

"Sir!"

Henle grew angry. He thundered, "That's my decision!"

Gilbert tugged at his sleeve. "You've got what you wanted. Don't make things worse by arguing with him like this in public."

Stephen bowed to Henle. "I'm sorry, my lord. By your leave."

Both Stephen and Gilbert backed away, then turned and marched out of the hall.

In the sunshine of the inner bailey, Gilbert began chuckling.

"What are you laughing at?" Stephen said irritably.

"You and Henle. I thought he was going to burst when you asked for bail."

"Well, I can do that, can't I?"

"I suppose you can. You know, that's going to be the biggest black eye I've ever seen, and I've seen more than a few."

"That's hard to imagine for a man who's led such a peaceful life."

"Oh, not that peaceful, at least when I was a boy. Come on, let's go tell Peter he's a free man."

"Not so free yet."

"He will be, eventually. I've no doubt Valence will release him. He won't love you for it, though."

They crossed through the gate into the outer bailey.

The castle gaol used to be in one of the corner towers of the inner bailey, but some years ago it had been relocated to a wooden structure hugging the east wall. As they cut through the crowd, which was now substantial, Gilbert said, "You know, you've made enemies of two of the most powerful men in this part of the county, three if you count Fitzsimmons. Not bad for only a month on the job."

"Do you think Sir Geoff will be angry?"

"I daresay. He likes things calm. But don't worry about being discharged. It'll blow over, and he'd rather have someone else do his work. Sir Geoff likes his meat pies more than work, especially our sort."

The gaol had one door bearing a large iron latch and padlock and barred windows. The guard occupied a stool by the door. His job was to keep the curious away from the prisoners rather than to keep the prisoners in. He stood as they reached the door. He hesitated, uncertain whether to order them away, but Stephen was so obviously a knight, although a badly battered one, that he wasn't sure how to proceed. "Can I help you, sirs?"

Gilbert said, "There's been a change of plan. Bromptone isn't to hang today. We've come here to tell him."

"I'm not supposed to let anyone talk to the prisoners," the guard said.

Gilbert drew himself up. It was like watching a bantam rooster ready for a fight. "This man is Stephen Attebrook, the deputy coroner. I don't think you are in a position to refuse him."

"Sorry, sir."

"No offense taken, my good man. You may resume your seat."

"Thank you, sir."

Gilbert called through the little barred square in the door, "Peter! Peter Bromptone! Can you hear me?"

After a time, a muffled voice called back. "I hear you!" The voice broke, as if in a sob.

"This is Stephen Attebrook and Gilbert Wistwode. We've good news," Gilbert called through the grill. "We've found Baynard's killer! You'll not be hanged today!"

"Oh, dear God!" Peter sobbed. "You must hurry! Amicia! She means to kill herself rather than live past this day! Find her! Hurry! Please hurry!"

"She said what?" Gilbert and Stephen shouted simultaneously.

"She was just here!" Peter called out from the dim recesses of the gaol. "The guard wouldn't let her talk to me, but I heard her call out through the door. She said that we'd be together in Heaven this afternoon. I'm sure she means to kill herself!"

Stephen whirled about, his one good eye scanning the crowd. That one eye and a thundering headache that pounded with every beat of his heart made it impossible to see clearly. "You go to the right, I'll take the left. We must find her!"

Gilbert nodded grimly and hurried away.

Stephen cast about as he strode quickly among the crowd, looking from one woman to another. The thought of Amicia's beautiful face, still and pale in death, was chilling. More and more people were streaming though the gate to the town and the bailey was rapidly filling with people. It seemed as though the entire town had turned out for the hanging, which it probably had. Even apprentices had been given time off for the spectacle. But he did not see her.

He turned a full circle, frantic with worry.

Then a movement above on the wall caught his eye. A figure had just disappeared at the door to a tower that sat at the junction of the walls to the inner and outer baileys. It had not been a soldier's figure, but a woman, fleetingly seen.

Stephen wasn't sure. But he ran for the wooden steps leading up to the wall walk just the same.

Awkward and slow with his bad foot and weighted with mail, it seemed forever before he was at the foot of the stairs. He lumbered up them two at a time and rushed for the tower.

He nearly knocked down a soldier inside the tower.

"Was there a woman?" Stephen gasped. "Did you see her?"

The soldier gaped and pointed to the door to the right, which opened onto the wall of the inner bailey.

Stephen ran through the door. Just ahead, at the door to the old keep, a flurry of skirts were disappearing. Stephen ran into the keep.

No one was there on the floor he entered, but he heard the scraping of footsteps in the stairwell above. He struggled after them.

They led up and up. It seemed so far and he moved in slow motion.

At last, he emerged onto the roof. It was deserted, except for the woman. Even before she turned, he knew it was Amicia. Her rich brown hair carefully woven into a single braid that fell to her thighs, that proud but demure carriage, and that long neck were unmistakable.

"Amicia!" he called out. "Wait."

She half turned and hesitated as he started toward her. Then she jumped quickly to the parapet between two teeth of the crenelations.

"Don't come any closer," Amicia said. "I shall jump if you take another step."

"Suicide is a sin, Amicia," Stephen said. He edged half a step closer.

"God is forgiving," she said. "He told me so last night."

Stephen noticed that she had a small white cross, carved from bone, in her hands. "There is no need! I've found who killed Baynard! Peter won't be hanged!"

She spat, "So you say. I've seen the way you look at me. You'd let him die, thinking you could have me when he's gone."

"Come see him now. You'll know I'm not lying."

Just then there was a roar from the crowd. A sheriff's bailiff had unlocked the door to the gaol. Four prisoners rather than three emerged. Guards led them toward the scaffold. The thief struggled and had to be carried. The robbers capered, despite the fact their hands were bound behind them, accepting the screams of the crowd as if they were applause. Peter, who came last, stumbled as if in a daze.

Amicia regarded the spectacle with dull eyes. "So I see, Stephen. Yet there he is."

Stephen pressed against the parapet. He shouted that there had been a mistake, that Peter was not supposed to hang. But the clamor from the crowd was so great that he could not be heard.

Indecision griped him. Events were moving so quickly that if he ran to save Peter, there was a good chance he would be too late. If he tried and failed, Amicia surely would throw herself off the tower. He could lose both of them. He couldn't make up his mind what to do. The agony was overwhelming.

The four prisoners reached the scaffold. Stools had been placed for each of them beneath the nooses and they were lifted upon them. The nooses were put around their necks and tightened. Henle was there, his big square figure unmistakable. He spoke to the crowd, but though his lips moved the uproar was so constant that it was doubtful anyone could hear what he said.

A commotion roiled the crowd. Gilbert had seen the mistake and was forcing his way through, but the press was thick and no one wanted to yield his place. A bagpipe began to wail. Amicia drew closer to the edge. Her eyes were on Peter down below. Stephen crept closer to her, gathering himself for a lunge.

Henle gestured to one of his bailiffs, who kicked the stool from beneath the thief. The man dropped to the end of his rope and began to swing. His legs jerked and thrashed as he struggled against the noose. Henle gestured again, and the bailiff kicked the stool from beneath one of the robbers. He dropped and swung, thrashing in death like the thief. His brother watched his brother dying with a sneer on his face. He spat onto the face of the bailiff, who kicked the stool from beneath his feet without waiting for an order from Henle.

The bailiff moved to Peter.

Amicia gathered herself to leap.

Stephen was still three paces from her — an impossible distance. He took a step. She didn't see him. Her eyes were on Peter. She was going to time her leap to the moment the bailiff kicked the stool.

Henle raised his hand.

Gilbert broke through the edge of the crowd. He caught Henle's hand. He shouted into Henle's ear. Henle shook him off and raised his hand again.

The bailiff kicked the stool, and Peter dropped to the end of his rope.

Amicia stepped into space.

Stephen dove and grasped her about the legs.

Her momentum nearly carried him with her. He halted their descent only by hooking his thighs against the edge of the wall. They both hung head down. Stephen's head pounded so that he thought he might pass out.

For a moment, Amicia was still. Then she began to thrash and kick. He could not believe how heavy and strong such a slight girl could be. Stephen's grip began to loosen. She slipped down, first an inch, then two, then another. He was going to lose her, and it must be fifty feet to the grass of the inner castle ditch. She could not survive such a fall.

A child at the rear of the crowd must have heard Amicia's cries. The little girl tugged her mother's sleeve, and pointed. The mother sounded the alarm, and people turned away from the hanging to watch the nearer spectacle, which was more odd and interesting. It wasn't every day people got to see a girl hang upside down from a castle tower with her shirt falling about her head and her legs on full display.

Amicia got a leg loose and put the foot on Stephen's shoulder. She pressed with all her might. Stephen caught the ankle as her other leg came free, then caught that ankle too.

He should have been able to haul up her now, but Stephen was so spent that he could not do it.

She was going to fall.

He had failed.

Then four men at the rear of the crowd ran forward with a blanket on which their family had been having a picnic. They held out the blanket beneath Amicia.

They shouted to Stephen to let her go.

It was a long way and they might miss.

He couldn't hold on any longer. His fingers were numb.

He released her.

Amicia hung in space for a moment, as if suspended by an invisible wire. Then she plunged, slowly at first, gradually gathering speed. Her skirt flapped back about her legs, and the sound of the skirt snapping in the wind seemed to Stephen to be the only noise in the entire bailey, for the whole crowd had gone silent.

She struck the clot of men holding the blanket with an audible thump and they all collapsed in a heap.

Stephen pulled himself up and leaned on his arms against the wall. Amicia's face was a blot as white as clean linen, then a wave of heads bending over her to provide aid obscured his view.

He looked to see what had become of Peter. To his relief, no body dangled at Peter's place. Someone had cut him down.

Gilbert was bulling his way through the throng toward the wall beneath Stephen, followed closely by the slender Peter, the noose still round his neck.

When Peter reached Amicia, the crowd drew back. He knelt by her.

"Amicia," Peter croaked, "what have you done? Don't die, for God's sake, don't die!"

"Ah," she said. Stephen heard that much clearly. She touched Peter's face. And smiled wanly.

Stephen failed to see or hear anything more, for his knees gave way and he sat down hard, nearly bumping his chin on the wall on the way down.

After a few moments, he got unsteadily to his feet and went down to the bailey.

Gilbert was waiting for him at the base of the wall. By the time Stephen reached him, a litter had been found for Amicia, and there were more than enough volunteers willing to carry her back to the Broken Shield. In the hubbub, Henle had forgotten to re-cage his prisoner, for Peter clutched her hand through the gate. What happened beyond that Stephen couldn't see.

A few people remaining in the bailey clapped Stephen on the back and offered congratulations at his deed. They called him a hero, but he didn't feel like one. There was no sense of triumph, no elation of victory that heroes must feel. There was only immense fatigue and relief that he had not failed after all, mingled with a twinge of dread over where he must stand now with Henle and Valence.

"I've put out the story that she slipped while watching the hanging," Gilbert said. "It's best left that way."

Stephen nodded.

Gilbert took him by the arm and led him toward the gate to the inner bailey, where they'd left their horses. "Come along, my boy," Gilbert said, "let's get a plaster on you. You could frighten children with that face."

"She'll live, you think?"

"I expect so. Broke the arm of one of the men who caught her, but she's broken nothing herself. She's just badly shaken."

"That's good. I'm glad."

"I wonder how Fitzsimmons is doing with that arm of his. I'm not sure it wasn't broken after all."

"Whiling his afternoon away till nightfall, I expect. He'll be gone not long after it's dark, I'm sure."

Gilbert looked hard at Stephen. "You want him to run."

Stephen shrugged.

Gilbert's eyes narrowed even more. "No, it's not Fitzsimmons, is it. But that boy, Edgar — why?"

Stephen looked uncomfortable. After a long pause, when it became clear that Gilbert would wait until sundown for an answer, he said, "I would have done the same thing in his place. It was feud. He had no choice."

"That's a devil of a way for an officer of the crown to behave!"

"A man who buries dead men in his latrine has no room for complaint."

Gilbert shushed him. "Not so loud, for God's sake!"

They reached their horses, which were still tethered to a post outside the hall's front door. They mounted and rode into the outer bailey.

As they emerged onto High Street, Stephen said, "I think I'll go for a bath. It's been a whole week. Care to join me?"

"Don't mind if I do."

Made in the USA
Middletown, DE
14 March 2022